I0575128

Astra Woman
And the Great Galactic Goodbye

by Wade D. Brown

Probabilities Publishing

ISBN: 979-8-9919780-0-2
Library of Congress Control Number: 2024926287

COVER ART collage design by Wade D. Brown
from images courtesy of Pixabay.com
compiled and edited using Canva online

artist credits:
galaxy — artist CursedQueen
futuristic city — artist DGS studios
woman — artist rbribella12
dog — artist Alanajordan
sphere — OpenClipart-Vector

Dedication: To the real-life Jeanne and Gates (and Laffy and all other four-pawed best friends) who inspired these characters. May your Astral adventures lead you through young-hearted heights and flights of fancy, and always end up in big playful yards.

Note to the reader: for official galactic accuracy, Jeanne's name is pronounced "Jeannie."

Chapter 1

"They've done it again!" the voice said in Jeanne's head—a familiar if vaguely non-human personality on her private comm.

"Done what again?" Jeanne responded irritably.

The voice began to sound agitated. "Our worst nightmare!"

"You'll have to be more specific. I have lots of nightmares. Comes with the job." Ambassador Jeanne (mid-level Gray rank), preparing for her official meeting with delegates from the slime world of Gu'gundrea—a world known to outsiders by the pejorative "Goo," though no one dared call it that in their presence—had her mind preoccupied at the moment trying to squeeze her elderly but dignified form into a thick and rubbery life-support suit, specially designed to protect against the highly alkaline liquid-mucous environment the squirmy Gu'gundreans lived in. As Galactic Sector 3,719,022 Ambassador for the Alien Council of Goodwill, it was Jeanne's job to maintain cordial relations, good feelings, upbeat attitudes, and deliver welcome baskets to all sentient lifeforms in her assigned Sector.

"You know...*it!* It it *it!*" Through his growing anxiety, Jeanne's genetically-augmented canine companion couldn't help conveying his loyalty and affection, an undercurrent of friendly warmth relayed mind-to-mind via their implanted cyber-neural amplifiers.

Jeanne ruffled the short yellow-brown fur above his floppy ears. "Calm down, Gates. That's a good boy." Despite his expanded intellect—arguably greater than many humans—Gates could be a bit over-eager and unrelenting like a...well, like a dog with a bone. She gave up on her suit's uncooperative molecular fasteners. "Call hotel services, would you? I need to have this suit let out a little in the hips."

Obediently if impatiently, Gates sent a comm request to the room service AI of the Stellar-Hyatt Hotel—number 61,832 of the outer-galactic-arm regional hostelries, city of Lusteer, capital of the planet Lystrom Two, center of a local system of some seven-thousand loosely-confederated stars.

Then he nuzzled her leg for attention. As a highly-trained clandestine service canine in the Special Partner Operations and Techniques (SPOT) Division, with top-secret enhancements not available commercially, it was his job to provide her with vital intelligence and any other needed information.

"All right, fine." Jeanne pulled her arms free from her suit. "Show me what's got you so worked up."

Gates wagged his tail. "This is a secure narrow-beam comm squirt I just received from Intelligence Division, priority alpha-one-slash-omega." From his collar he projected an image in the air: a small globular galaxy, uniform in structure and unremarkable. As they watched, the galaxy began to shrink, and—impossibly—collapsed in on itself. In a matter of seconds it reduced to a small bright ball that flared briefly, then winked out—gone.

Jeanne blinked. "Holy higher chakras! That's not...."

"Not the same anomaly recorded by spy ships two months ago, no. This is a new one."

Jeanne felt the hair on her neck rise. "Another entire galaxy disappeared? I wouldn't exactly call that an 'anomaly.' It defies physics! Not to mention any stretch of logic or reason. Was it inhabited?"

"Unclear. Should I fetch more information?"

"Yes, fetch boy! Go get it."

Gates's ears perked up. "Retrieving now from Intelligence Division. Okay, fortunately not inhabited. Analysis suggests both anomalies were tests conducted in secret far out in an area of unlivable space."

"That's a relief!" Jeanne's brow darkened. "Tests? What kind of tests? A weapon of some kind!"

"That's the Intel AI's best guess. Some device that warps space-time on a colossal scale, able to fold mass and dimension in on itself, vanishing into zero-dimensional unexistence while exceeding space-time relativistic limits, although this video was time-compressed by several factors—we're seeing in a few seconds what really took two weeks."

"Unbelievable! How are we able to even see such a thing at all?"

"The spy ships use sub-quantum dimensional scanning. Same principle used in our trans-space communications and starship FTL drives, which taps into hidden or 'curled-up' extra dimensions at the sub-quantum scale, uncurls them so to speak. Then while they're still in a quantum uncertainty state they become entangled with our ordinary 4-D space-time, a superposed state of neither here nor there you might say. At that point we can recollapse all the dimensions and let everything rebound to normal—but with a slight shift in our perspective or position. That's how we bypass normal speed-of-light barriers and experience these things pretty much in real-time. Not to get too technical about it."

"Yeah, let's not do that." Jeanne sank onto the edge of the hotel suite's air cloud bed—just air molecules that congealed into a coherent but yielding springy lattice, a nearly-invisible cushion that conformed perfectly to her every body part. She let the luxurious sensation cradle her for a moment, calling on her years of meditation training to calm her mind and emotions.

It didn't work. "It's monstrous!" she exploded. "Who would destroy entire galaxies? And what would be the point?"

Gates gave a doggie shrug. "We have to assume the perpetrators intend it as a message to the rest of us. Or a deterrent. Just to show they can do it—and that no galaxy is safe."

"So then everyone else will have to fall in line with whatever they want or be wiped out of existence! Vile and evil!" She shook her head. "But it still doesn't make sense. How many galaxies could they destroy before it becomes self-defeating!"

"Mmm...a lot actually. You know how many trillions of galaxies there are in the universe. That's more than all the grains of sand on Earth's beaches. Scoop out a bone hole of beach sand—or a handful in your case—and fling it in the ocean. Would those grains be missed?"

Jeanne shuddered. "That's a scary notion!"

"Yes. But to some, apparently diabolically appealing. Although you humans have a twisted sense of humor. Some jokers in Intel Division are calling this new weapon the Great Galactic Goodbye Gizmo."

"*Not* funny!" Jeanne turned to stare out the plasteel transparent wall at the towering silver spires, ribbon bridges and golden domes of the capital city, aircars and small flyers whizzing in sunlight like multi-colored glittering insects. From the lofty height of their hotel room she could see beyond the city's edge to the sprawling parks, the verdant nature preserves and pristine waterways stretching to the mountains in the distance. She thought of the other cities and lands and teeming people around the planet—and the millions of other planets and civilizations strewn throughout the galaxy. Then she imagined it all gone, winked out of existence like that video image.

Deeply shaken, she faced her canine collaborator again. "Do we have any idea of their next step?"

Gates tilted his head, requesting and processing data. "The analysts believe these first tests were just about perfecting the weapon. Next they'll try a more visible demonstration to make their point, a galaxy in our local cluster."

"An inhabited one!"

"Yes."

"How much time before that happens?"

"They expect it will take a while to set up for the next one. Sub-quantum dimensional transport is fast, but not instantaneous, especially at intergalactic distances. And they anticipate an announcement of demands first."

"Demands. So we still have a little time to stop them, then. Does Intel Div have any idea who's behind it?"

"No. Although...this is interesting. They did trace a brief trans-space comm thread just before each of the two events. A signal originating from—get this—right here in this city."

"What?" Jeanne's expression widened. "So *that's* why they secure comm squirted us."

"Yes, we're the only covert team already on site. Looks like this is a job for Astra Woman."

"Right!" Jeanne stood and mentally recited a code in her cyber-neural net, activating swarms of organic nanobots tagged uniquely to her genome that immediately went to work on her cells, generating a revitalization and energy surge that coursed through her body, sweeping aside outward manifestations of age and infirmity, restoring youthful vigor and resilience. In a few heartbeats she had transformed from the respected elder statesperson into a lithe, strong and supple twenty-something in the peak of health—no longer the distinguished ambassador for the Alien Council of Goodwill, but now a superbly-honed clandestine agent for the Council's super-secret Civil Protection and Astral Security Division, ready for action. Code name: Astra Woman.

"Wait!" Gates trotted in front of her. "Are you forgetting? You have to meet with the Gu'gundrean delegation in half and hour."

"Ah. Almost forgot. Ambassadorial duties first, secret spy stuff afterwards." She reversed the transformation process, returning to her more mature and reserved appearance, then gazed unhappily at the alkaline-protecting life-support suit, still half-on and half-off. She sighed. "I guess I'm just not real keen on the idea of swimming around in slimy goo in this get-up."

Gates gave a doggie chuckle and a tail wag. "Now *that's* funny!"

* * * *

Ambassador Jeanne, bedecked in stately gray robes with gold lapel and sleeve embroidering, strode from the hotel's lower-lobby concourse through double doors to meet the Gu'gundrean delegation, and stopped in surprise. "The hotel swimming pool?" Her words echoed within the Olympic-sized enclosure. Abruptly she got a whiff of the horrendous stench and covered her mouth and nose, eyeing the viscous, greenish, unsettlingly swirling contents of the pool.

Beside her, the local consulate assigned to accompany her, sub-attaché Roingroing, wheezed, "It issss the only recsssseptacle capaciousss enough to housssse the Gu'gundreansss." A bulbous Spraang species from the planet Andreon Four in the Small Outer Inner Cluster,

Roingroing looked like a tough elastic sphere about two-feet in diameter and vibrant pink. Mostly filled with gas, the Spraangs locomoted by bouncing in the air and shooting out a sticky pseudopod at their target, then pulling themselves forward—disconcerting if *you* were the pseudopod's target, but somewhat comical otherwise. Humans had given them the nickname "Dodge-balls"—again pejoratively, and again not to their faces, even though they didn't *have* faces.

Roingroing bounced a little further into the pool room, opened a skin slit slightly and expelled internal gas to vibrate in airy mimicry of human speech. To Jeanne it sounded like someone squeaking through a leaky car tire. "We are sssstill conssstructing a larger facsssility for their embasssy, but that'sss going to take sssome time. Meanwhile thisss isss the bessst we can do."

Jeanne tried not to breathe the fumes coming off the voluminous concentration of mucous in the pool. She was glad Gates didn't have to be here for this part, but had gone off on his own information-gathering romp. Although, come to think of it, he might actually enjoy this.

"Smells like vomit," she remarked.

"It'sss sssnot."

"What?"

"I sssaid, it'sss not. Vomit isss acidic, the Gu'gundrean environment isss alkaline. They're oppositesss."

Jeanne grimaced at the Spraang species' infamous reputation for literalness, which could often lead to humorous—or annoying—misunderstandings. "My nose doesn't know the difference."

"Yesss, human olfactory capabilitiesss are sssadly lacking. Now, when you sssink into the pool don't be dissscouraged by the ssshocksss and pricklesss you'll experiencsse. The Gu'gundreansss communicate by electrical currentsss. And it ssseems the ssstronger the shocksss the more they like you. We've desssigned your sssuit as an insssulator, which ssshould ssscreen out anything lethal."

"Thoughtful of you. Wait—*should* screen out?"

"We're ssstill getting to know them. Asss an ambasssador I'm sssure you're aware of uncsssertaintiesss in any negotiationsss."

"Yeah," she mumbled under her breath, "I just wasn't expecting my *life* to be one of those uncertainties."

"What did you sssay?"

"Nothing." She slipped off her robe, exposing her protective suit, then pulled its rubbery helmet onto her head and fastened the neck seal. As she did so a long translucent eel-like creature the same color as the goo broke the surface of the pool and looked at her—or seemed to since it had no eyes—then ducked back under. "How exactly do I talk to them? *I* don't communicate electrically."

"Your sssuit doesss. Teamsss of linguisssstsss and computer analysssts have been working on a language transsslation for sssix monthsss. Jussst ssspeak normally, and the transsslation algorithm will hopefully get mossst of your ideasss acrosss."

"Hopefully? Most? You're just filled with reassurance, aren't you?"

"No, I'm filled with a nitrogen-methane-hydrogen-carbon-oxygen gassseousss mix. I don't undersssstand your missstaken referencsssse."

"Never mind. We'd better begin. Don't want to keep their delegation waiting." She knelt at the pool's edge, started to swing her legs over the side—when a rope-like translucent tentacle whipped out of the goo, wrapped around her waist, and yanked her bodily into the slimy fluid.

As she splurged into the depths of the warm glop,

electrical prickles raced up and down her limbs and body, sharp tiny jolts with occasional more powerful jagged shocks, accompanied by a background of tingling static caresses and fingers of DC energy. But they didn't feel random or uncontrolled. These were patterned, regular pulses of intelligent sensing.

She got hold of herself and stifled her instinctive panic—they wouldn't knowingly harm a Goodwill ambassador. She oriented herself in the thick goopy soup. Not so bad after the initial shock—no pun intended. She could swim a little, or at least hold station.

Light filtered down into the hazy medium in soft beams, like looking through a swimming pool full of pale green body-wash gel (very bad-smelling body-wash gel). A small eel-like critter slithered under her armpit and wriggled away to hide behind a larger one that floated quietly in front of her. Mama and baby? She stayed still, not wanting to appear threatening.

As she grew used to the womb-like surroundings and constant electric prickling, more of those larger eel-beings gathered around her. Giant gummy-worms, her imagination thought childishly—then she chastised herself for such an inappropriate image. These were sophisticated beings! Anyway, some of them changed shape into bloated blobs or pulsing jellyfish-like mushroom-balloons, hinting at their true malleable and gelatinous nature.

She became aware of her translator humming and crackling, converting some of those staticky signals or electric chatter into human language:

Crackle hum "Time waits...we grow..." *Crackle hum* "More...."

Okay, so the translator wasn't perfected yet. "Hello," Jeanne tried. "Greetings. We wish you well."

Crackle hum "Greet...more...."

Hmm. She tried again. "I bring felicitations from the Council of Goodwill."

Crackle hum "Greet."

She waited, but nothing else came, just lots of static.

Well, this wasn't going especially well. How did they ever get these guys to come here in the first place with this kind of crappy communication? She would have to have a serious talk with someone about this. All right, once more. "We welcome you—"

"Welcome!" *Crackle hum.* A surge of energy assaulted her.

She caught her breath and tried to calm her heart at the unexpected salvo. Her suit compensated, increasing its electrical resistance and upping her O_2.

Careful, she told herself. This could get out of hand. That's a lot of energy out there!

Wait a second. Energy?

Yes! Why not? When words failed....

She centered herself, quieting her mind, seeking a deeper understanding beyond the words, feeling her life-force focus and gather within as she'd often practiced in her meditations and healing energy work. Familiar sensations flowed through her—all part of her ambassadorial skill-set and a requirement for advancement to the senior levels in this most inter-relational of professions.

More self-assured now, she visualized her inner power radiating from her, blending with the surrounding alien energies. "I give you good energy!" she said expansively.

The electrical tingles contacting her skin seemed to respond, to merge with her own energy, interfacing and amplifying, then redirecting to stream outward into the conductive medium around her.

The goo-beings drew back as if startled. Several swirled

around each other, evidently convening. Then they turned back to her and their chatter increased. The electrical fingers reversed once again to race over her skin even more strongly.

Crackle hum "Energy...good...more...."

Was that an acknowledgment or a request? A bit hesitantly, she accepted the incoming energy flow and, when it didn't seem to harm her, embraced it and returned it in kind.

As she did, a field began to build between her and the goo-beings, a glow of underwater coronal fire—tongues of blue St.-Elmo's lightning that lapped and danced, arcing outward and playing back and forth between her and them, a strange ethereal communication of pure energy. She'd never experienced anything quite like it.

The field continued to build, and where others might be afraid at the unfamiliarity and intensity of this other-worldly discharge, she encouraged it, contributed to it, cherished it.

And now, carried on those conductive waves she sensed something more than just energy, something purposeful and meaningful: the thoughts and minds themselves, the feelings, experiences, personalities—alien though they were. It surpassed language, transcended communication. It became a sharing, an identity, a oneness, a wholeness, a *rightness*.

She saw then...no, she *knew*...what they knew, what they truly were: the comforting sense of family and home and a world of boundless gooey seas, and freedom and joy and leaping play, and reverence for prior untold generations and traditions, and the prospect of endless continuing futures....

In return she wanted to share her own far-flung community's diverse history and hopes, its shortcomings and failures—both it's recurrent self-destructiveness and simultaneous great capacity for cooperation, and ultimately it's banding together through the Council of Goodwill to build a better future for all.

But then something else came through from her hosts—a worry, a dark spot, something *not* family and home, something alien and threatening. It touched a similar place in her own mind, a jarring synchrony of apprehension, a repellent recognition of the same dark worry....

No! She gasped and recoiled, then lurched away, clawing up and out of the pool, breaking the connection. She pulled herself and several liters of dripping goo onto hard aquamarine tiles, then collapsed on a colorful starfish-and-dolphin mosaic, breathing hard.

Roingroing bounced over, extended a concerned pseudopod to help steady her. "Are you sssstable? How did thingsss go?"

Jeanne pulled her suit's hood off. "I'm fine. I think. Things went—a little crazy."

"Crazsssy? Can you be more sssspecific?"

"Well, better than expected at first. But unexpected, too."

"Ah. That'sss to be exssspected, I exssspect."

Jeanne stared at the living goo, glad to be free of that one dark horrifying thought she'd experienced. Yet at the same time she felt let down upon losing that total embracing energy connection.

But she'd seen enough. More than enough. She shivered. They *knew*. That was the dark worry they'd communicated—they knew about the Great Galactic Goodbye Gizmo!

But exactly *what* they knew shook her to the core.

*   *   *   *

"What do you mean, it's been tampered with?" Jeanne slipped on her gray ambassador's tunic and slacks, the informal everyday ones with tastefully understated blue piping along hems and seams. The hotel room's ventilators kicked into high gear to counteract the residual smell from her goo suit (that's how she thought of it now, even though it had been thoroughly power washed and de-gunked—it's official designation, the Alkalinity Protection Environmental suit or APE suit didn't really appeal to her). The AI released more of her requested lilac and frangipani potpourri into the air.

Gates sniffed at her suit's limp helmet, now lying on the floor, probed it with cyber diagnostics. "What I mean is the translation software, while not flawless, ought to have worked quite well. For reasons unknown your translator was...defective. That's highly unlikely to have happened by itself. It had to have been tampered with."

"You're saying someone *deliberately* sabotaged my negotiations with the Gu'gundreans!"

"It smells that way. Did you at least have a chance to give them their welcome basket?"

"Of course. Though I'm not sure if slime beings are into mini muffins, dried fruits and boutique cheeses. Any idea who arranged the sabotaging?"

"No. Whoever did it was exceptionally good. They left no traces, physical or cyber."

Jeanne stewed. "Well, the joke's on them. Without language in the way I could actually make a more direct connection with the Gu'gundreans than I'd have been able to otherwise. And I learned something big...." She ran a furtive gaze over the room's characterless beige furnishings, the deceptively simple-looking automated lounge surfaces and self-mobile tables and lifeform-following lighting, all artfully masking many built-in service devices concealed in panels and cubbyholes—plenty of places to hide illegal surveillance gear. "Uh, what do you say we go for a walk."

She zipped up her tunic, its high-neck collar with the

golden-circle Council symbol pinned to one side and blue-star ambassador's pip on the other, both chafing under her chin. She pushed the collar down in absent irritation, but it popped right back up in defiance as it always did.

Gates jumped eagerly to his feet and dashed for the door.

Jeanne followed him into the hall and they rode the bullet elevator down nine-hundred-and-twenty floors to the main lobby—a stomach-churning drop—finally stepping out onto the hotel's ground floor transfer and loading loop, where they waved off a flock of autocabs and flitty-flyers, even avoided the moving walkways and robo-cycles and more leisurely and expensive reclinable hoverchairs. A "Dodge-ball" narrowly missed them as it bounded past, yanked along by its whip-like pseudopod. Scores of other creatures of all sizes, types, and arrangements of limbs—or lack thereof—jostled by on the busy boulevards leading into the heart of the city, where soaring and shiny buildings of inspired architecture promised all the diversions and rewards of civilization.

Instead they turned away, following a more discrete trail they'd mentally marked out earlier as part of Astra Woman's persona, a back route leading to an old-quarter side street that angled off into less-well-traveled sections of the city.

A sensor noted their deviation from normal traffic, read Jeanne's body type and features, selected from among fifty-five billion most-likely languages, projected a flashing bright-orange holo-notice in the air in front of her and loudly announced: "Warning! You are leaving the secure sections of the city. Civil services, public amenities, and personal safety cannot be guaranteed beyond this point. Please return to the customary patrolled areas. Warning! You are leaving the secure sections of the city...."

Jeanne ignored the quite sensible advice and pushed on

right through the glowing roadsign. Soon they entered an area of spottily-maintained streets and crumbling sidewalks dusty and dry in the sun, past little off-the-grid apartment buildings, off-the-beaten-path shops, and off-the-books taverns and stim-inns, a neighborhood once probably quaint and picturesque but now ancient and sagging and paint-peeled and many-times patched. But also happily free of public monitoring cameras and other snooping devices.

Naturally, that also provided the ideal refuge for shady-looking characters, some of whom lurked in doorways and alley mouths, like one square-bodied, six-legged Hougranian that tracked them with half of its eighteen eyestalks, its gray bulk clothed in ratty Space Mechanics and Loaders Union coveralls with the sleeves torn off, a number of badly-regenerated scars showing on its thick hide, a highly-addictive and illegal zoom-stick hanging from its bloated purple lips. As they passed, it swiveled all but five of its eye stalks back to flirt with its partner, a male of the species: a dirty-brown and sharp-toothed fur ball about six inches in diameter perched on a chipped window sill.

Gates glanced around in defensive alertness. He had a throaty growl locked and loaded, ready for release should any of these unsavory types come close.

Jeanne seemed only half aware of any potential danger, her mind absorbed by something more weighty.

"Well," Gates said at last. "Are you going to tell me what's got *you* so wound up, now?"

Jeanne looked up and down the street, checked the sky for spy drones. "All right. Make sure we're on private secure circuit."

"We've been on it since you got back from your little swim. Full covert protocol: near-field transmission only, narrow-beam with auto-target lock, random frequency switching, multiple-layer scrambling, no recording, active eavesdropping detection and dynamic defense with squeal jamming. Of course, that also means I'm disconnected from all my usual comm sources."

"You know, for peaceable representatives of the Council of Goodwill we sure don't seem to be all that trusting, do we?"

"Hey, if life was perfect they wouldn't need us."

"Ah...good point." She lifted a hand to formulate her thoughts. "Well, it's hard to put into words—and hard to believe—what the Gu'gundreans showed me. You see, because they communicate by energy fields instead of sound or sight, they can sense certain things other beings normally can't. They can sort of 'see' into people's minds, when those people are in their environment, in their goo. So the first ones to contact them—the exploration team, the translators, the Council's initial envoys, the embassy secretaries and attachés—all unknowingly gave the Gu'gundreans more information than they realized, even though it took the Gu'gundreans some time to process and convert that information into something they could make sense of. Anyway, it turns out one of those Council envoys had a secret. A huge secret, a dark secret. A secret she tried to keep not only from the Gu'gundreans but even from other members of the Goodwill Council—"

"Hold!" Gates halted tensely. His body stiffened and his tail elevated. "We're being stalked."

"We are?"

"Behind that trash bin across the street. Someone wearing a shadow cloak. They've been following us for the last half a block."

"You're sure?"

"Shadow cloaks aren't easy to come by, even on the black

market. Do you think anyone from this part of town can afford one?"

Jeanne peered at the old dented, greasy green garbage receptacle. She didn't see anything out of the ordinary. But then a shadow cloak would only be visible when the individual under it moved. "You know, it may not have been entirely prudent of me to wear my ambassador's togs out here so publicly. Let's keep going."

As they continued on she ventured a glance back. Was that a slight shifting of shadows by the trash bin? She looked for a place to duck into.

There. A recessed doorway in a decaying shingle-sided brown apartment building ahead. They hurried toward it, stepped quickly within the shallow enclosure amid smells of damp dirt and mildew.

Jeanne peeked back around the doorway's edge, pressing against coarse sandpapery old siding. For a moment she saw nothing unusual, then a wavery flicker of movement crossing the street toward them.

She pulled back. Time to put her Astra Woman alter ego to work. She scooted further into the recess and silently invoked the mental code that would begin her transformation.

As the energizing rush of metamorphosis flooded through her, she shed her ambassador's tunic and slacks and hung them with care on the building's rusty and broken doorknob, brushing a little dust off the sleeves and back first. Her undergarment, now exposed, transmogrified itself from an apparently unexceptional gray, off-the-rack, Steady-Temp™ smart onesy into a highly-classified Civil Protection and Astral Security Division skin-hugging sens-suit, shiny black, with multiple defensive and spying capabilities.

"Getting close!" Gates growled (literally growled, both

out loud and in her head).

Jeanne—now Astra Woman—edged up beside him. Through her sens-suit she felt multiple vibrations in the air, heard the rustling and breathing of someone approaching— human, it sounded, or something close. "Get ready. We'll two-team him. Diversionary tactic A-one."

"Rrrrright!" As the stalker drew near, Gates sprang from their doorway, barking and nipping at the intruder's nearly-invisible cloak, scuttling around to the far side to aim the fellow away from Jeanne-Astra Woman.

It worked only partly. The guy was too well trained to fall for so simple a trick. Then again, he did need to take at least a basic defensive posture against this attacking dog.

With his attention divided Astra Woman lunged at him in a flying tackle, knocking his arms down and pinning them to his sides as her momentum carried them to the ground. One of the man's hands came free of his cloak holding a nasty multi-pronged pressure-activated projectile knife—two of its six blades went *spung* and whizzed past her head to thud into the wall of a nearby building. Astra Woman trapped the arm so the knife pointed away from her and wrapped her legs around his with her enhanced athletic muscle strength, then commanded her sens-suit to go rigid.

As the man struggled and rocked back-and-forth in that unyielding grip, Gates leaped in and grabbed the knife-wielding wrist in his mouth, growling dangerously.

"I suggest you let go of that," Astra Woman advised, "if you ever want to use that hand again."

The man dropped the weapon. Gates pawed it aside, then released the wrist and pulled the man's cloak from his head and face, revealing a human of indeterminate mixed ancestry no different than quadrillions of others. The fellow quit resisting. Calmly he said, "May I sit up now?"

"Depends," Astra Woman said. "Who sent you?"

That brought a grim smile. "You know I can't tell you that."

"Think again." She increased her sens-suit's constricting pressure.

The man groaned as several of his joints creaked. "Do your worst! I won't talk."

She eased her grip. "I actually believe you. What you may not know, but *you* should believe, is that I work for some very determined and not-so gentle people who can find out every little secret you have without breaking a sweat. Or even any of your bones."

"Oh, I know the ultra hush-hush Division you work for. And, yes, I'm sure they can do that. Which is why this has to end now."

"Don't try to get away!" She increased the pressure of her suit just slightly. "It won't work."

"I see that," he replied with a grimace. He took a moment to consider. "So we're at a stalemate. Problem is, the people I work for are even more relentless than yours...and quite a bit more ruthless, with no qualms about using methods even *I* don't want to think about. You're sure you can't just let me go? It would be a whole lot simpler. I'm harmless now."

"Not a chance, buster! I'm taking you in, and we *will* find out who you work for."

"I was afraid of that." He gave a sigh. "Too bad, I had such big dreams. Oh, well. 'The best-laid plans,' and all. It's been...interesting meeting you." With that his eyes rolled up in his head, his cheeks turned bright red and puffed out, and blood spurted from his nose and ears.

Reflexively Astra Woman let him go. The man sagged limply, little wisps of steam wafting off his skin.

"Nano-suicide!" she gasped. What a terrible fate: auto

destruct cooking him from the inside-out. Whoever he worked for must really be cold-blooded to do that to him! A shame, though. He seemed like he might actually be a pretty nice guy at heart—when you got past the homicidal tendencies.

Gates stood frozen at attention, head cocked upward and away.

"What is it, boy?" Astra Woman asked, "More danger?"

Gates shook himself like throwing off muddy water. "No. But I did intercept a coded comm squirt from this guy just before he died."

"Oh! He must have signaled whoever sent him! Did you trace it?"

"Yes. But you won't like who that is."

Astra Woman narrowed her eyes. "I already have a pretty good suspicion."

"You do? How?"

"Just tell me."

Gates hesitated, his head and tail drooping.

"Speak, boy!"

Gates slunk down, fearful of what he must say. "It's...Senior Goodwill Councilor, Leonore Squag!" He covered his face with his paws.

Astra Woman nodded gravely, her worst fears realized. "I thought so. That's what I was about to tell you before this guy showed up, what I learned from the Gu'gundreans. The people behind the Great Galactic Goodbye Gizmo—it's the Goodwill Council itself!"

Chapter 2

"More bad news." Gates gave a wary glance around. "My comm uplink just went offline."

Jeanne frowned. "Sure. They must have been using that to track us, but now that we're on to them they're severing our communication with HQ."

"Not just with them. The public circuits are down, too. Net traffic, everything."

Jeanne tried her own open channels. "That tears it. Wait—our private comms are still working!"

"Our near-field electronics and onboard individual tech weren't affected. Apparently the Council only managed to shut down our outside connections, thanks in no small part to our super-classified personal cyber defenses. Luckily that also means they can no longer track us the same way, either."

"That's something, I guess. Their own paranoia hurts them. So now we're cut off from our Agency resources, can't even report in—although come to think of it, that may not be particularly advisable anymore. I suspect we've been labeled persona non grata by now, or worse. I guess that's what happens when the people at the top are the rotten eggs."

"Yeah. I don't think I'd trust going back to the hotel, either."

"Good point. Darn it, I left some really good clothes and my best carry-on luggage in that hotel room. So we've got our wits and that's about all, then." She regarded the steaming remains of their would-be assassin, sent a look up and down the street. "You know, suddenly standing around out here doesn't seem all that healthy. Let's get moving."

"Where to?"

"For now, anywhere. Preferably not out in the open where satellites and surveillance drones can see us. Grab that fellow's shadow cloak, will you? Might come in handy."

Gates gathered up the garment which had powered down and become a plain-looking brown cloth, passed it to her. "What about your Ambassador uniform?"

"Better leave it. It would just draw attention." She rolled up the cloak and tucked it under one arm. Then she reversed her youthful rejuvenation—wouldn't do to keep that going too long, it could be energy draining and have other long-term costs she didn't care to experience.

Finally she returned her sens-suit to it's looser and unremarkable gray appearance and they set off watchfully, keeping as close to buildings and overhangs as possible.

"Is there anyone on this planet you can contact?" Gates asked.

"We only arrived here a few days ago, I hardly met anybody. I think I'd actually trust the Gu'gundreans after my 'close encounter' with them, but getting into their swimming pool without being spotted by some shady operative on the Council's payroll probably isn't going to happen. Besides, my goo suit is back in the hotel room with all our other stuff."

"True. And we don't know *who* exactly might be one of those shady operatives. Suddenly my trust in my fellow sentient creatures just dropped a few notches."

"Hmm. There might be one individual I'd consider trustworthy—or at least incapable of subterfuge, given his overly-literal nature."

Gates looked interested. "You mean...?"

"We need to get a message to sub-attaché Roingroing. He should be back at his consulate office by now."

"Uh, I don't think contacting him openly is an option anymore."

"No, but according to his office schedule he leaves for home promptly at 5:00 pm local. If we take that literally—and I'm pretty sure we should—that means *precisely* at 5:00 pm local. We'll have to catch him right when he comes out—if we can figure out how to get there from here in time."

"Calling up a map of...oh crap, I forgot they cut off my access to everything!"

"Everything cyber you mean. We just have start doing things old-school. *Really* old-school."

"Like walking everywhere?"

"And asking directions. And watching news casts for anything relevant—people used to have something called TV."

"I've heard of that. Outdated technology, isn't it?"

"Some of these taverns and eateries here in the old quarter might still have working hook-ups. A lot of their patrons can't afford the modern amenities we take for granted, like cyber-neural comms. If things go our way I'm thinking we might even find a physical computer terminal."

Gates cocked his head. "Now you're *really* talking ancient technology!"

"I'm open to better suggestions. If we can get onto the city's Tourism and Commerce e-center we can access a map of downtown, figure out how to get to Roingroing's consulate offices."

"You think he'd help us?"

"If we can convince him. He has contacts, access to high-level people. People *not* in the Goodwill Council."

Gates grew somber. "That's a start, I suppose. Then what?"

"We play it by ear. We have to expose the Council, or whatever rogue faction within the Council that's doing all this. Especially Senior Councilor Leonore Squag. I don't know how far Roingroing's influence extends, though, and I don't want to put him in unnecessary danger, either. But he may be able to help us somehow, through back channels."

"Back channels. I suspect we're about to become uncomfortably familiar with back channels! You realize this isn't going to be easy?"

"Easy, no." She blew out a breath. "This is big, Gates. Bigger than anything we've ever dealt with before."

* * * *

They walked—or trotted—on in silence then, hoping to find someplace with "old-school" computer access, preferably something in the black- or maybe gray-market range of legal shading that wouldn't reveal their presence to cyber cops or Council spies. They tried stopping a couple of the less-belligerent-looking citizens for hints and directions, finally got pointed to one of the stim-inns in the neighborhood.

Jeanne halted outside the questionable establishment and eyed the weathered green wooden storefront that hadn't been painted in a couple of decades, the boarded-over windows, the erratically flickering red holo sign above the yellowish door proclaiming in Galactic Trade Standard "Lo-Lo's Happy Time Lucky Place." A robo-eye beside the dented steel door swiveled and scanned them up and down. "What want?" a mechanical voice said, also in Galactic Trade Standard.

"Drinks," Jeanne responded. "News."

"Credit," the voice demanded.

This could be a problem, Jeanne thought, cut off as they were from their normal resources. Fortunately as an ambassador she'd been supplied for such emergencies with a number of payment methods, from electronic (no longer prudent, given their current on-the-lam status) to untrackable hard coin of the realm that should be accepted anywhere. She unsealed a thigh pocket and pulled out several of the latter, held them up to the robo-eye.

After a moment's inspection an electronic lock whirred and the door swung outward.

They stepped into a dimly-lit hall heavy with musty smells of stale perfume, incense, alcohol, and cloying vapors from who knows what other legal and illegal substances. Dark-curtained booths lined each side, flanking a few small tables in the center where three lone customers sat. A short bar occupied the far end—with a TV screen above it. They headed that way.

The three customers, aliens of widely-varying species, followed them suspiciously with their respective photo receptors.

A robo-attendant ran the bar, an archaic stainless torso-and-head affair rolling back and forth on a track attached to the back of the bar's countertop. One of its four arms placed a bottle on the wall behind it among dozens of other jugs, carafes, urns, small boxes, and miscellaneous bric-a-brac. Then it rotated to face the newcomers and slid toward them on its track. "Choice?" it asked. Up close it exhibited numerous scratches, dings, abrasions, and other scars from its long tenure at its job.

They took seats at two of the few bar stools, Gates hopping up on one next to Jeanne. She held the rolled-up shadow cloak in her lap for safekeeping, said, "I'll take a Stellar Sunset. And lime-coconut water for my friend."

"Does not register." The robo-attendant swept one of its arms at the assortment on the back wall. "Choose."

Well, no surprise they didn't serve classy drinks here. Jeanne looked over the offerings, pointed at a flask, not sure about any of these unfamiliar labels. The attendant rotated to retrieve the selection, poured a small glass.

She sniffed it, took a sample sip. Spicy, but not bad.

"Next." The attendant settled its optical sensors on Gates.

Gates spoke to Jeanne in her head. "Ask if they serve food. We haven't eaten in awhile, and might not have another chance anytime soon."

"Okay, but we can't linger. We have to make our date with Roingroing, and we're running out of afternoon." She spied a stack of menus at the end of the bar, gestured at it.

The robo-attendant slid down its rail-track, brought one back. Not knowing the hygiene of the kitchen here, they each picked something standard and prepackaged: Cosmo Farms friendly lab-grown meat and vegetable quick-dinners ("no animals were harmed in the making of this meal").

As their food heated, Jeanne made another request, trying to keep it simple. Trade Standard lingo was practical and basic by design, but this auto-server seemed to take that concept to a whole new level. "Uh, TV. Want news. Local."

That seemed phrased well enough to suit the robot's brain. It switched to a news channel.

But reports were pretty standard. The biggest story of the moment seemed to be first contact with the Gu'gundreans and speculations on how negotiations were going. Other than that, nothing out of the ordinary. And, most importantly, no "be-on-the-lookout" notices for any new fugitives or renegade Ambassadors with dogs.

"No news is good news," Gates opined. "So what's our play now?"

"Not sure yet. I'm still reeling from learning that our own Council, or some part of it, are the bad guys."

"Yeah. Kind of makes you question a few things—like everything you've always believed in."

They finished eating quickly and Jeanne inquired about a possible computer terminal.

"Booth one. Time limit. Fifteen minutes."

"Should be more than enough." She got up and turned to go.

A robo arm snaked out and blocked her way. "Pay now." An itemized bill glowed in weak green letters on the attendant's chest plate. A bit pricier than expected, but she dug in her thigh pocket for the payment, reflecting that they would need to be more frugal with their few remaining coins.

Behind booth one's curtain they found a barely-lit cubbyhole smelling unpleasantly of old unidentifiable body odors. A low padded bench folded down from one wall opposite a shelf where an ancient and much-cracked laptop sat. They crowded in and closed the curtain.

"What do you think, Gates?"

"I'm sensing a radio emission. I think they used to call it 'wi-fi.' I'll see if I can tap in. Yes...crude but manageable. Very slow, though."

"See if you can fetch that map."

"Let's see. City services, info page, points of interest. Here we go." A street map came up on the laptop's screen, scrolled sideways. "We want the Spraang consulate in the capitol plaza...there it is."

"Okay. Upload that."

"Uh, sorry, can't. No Agency uplink, remember? So no cyber storage. And my own onboard memory is about maxed out. I'm assuming you don't want me to delete any of the incriminating evidence I managed to save, like the video of that galaxy collapsing. Lots of data there."

"No, you're right. I guess we'll just have to memorize the city layout. I did say old-school, didn't I? You know, you'd think the Agency would have given *me* some extra memory capacity for situations like this."

"Don't be too hard on the tech geeks. Your sens-suit and rejuvenation take a *lot* of computing power. Not much left for anything else. That's why you've got me!" He gave a doggie grin.

"Yeah, you're such a good boy!" She scratched behind his ears. "And I don't suppose the techies ever imagined a situation like this. All right, find us a route between here and the consulate. Better make that a back-street route."

"On it." He highlighted a couple of possibilities. "But if we have to go by foot...I'm not sure we'll make it by 5:00 pm."

"We have to try. Give me a second to get this map oriented in my head. So...the capitol is over there, the consulate and diplomatic center not far from it, our hotel is back over *there*, and we're down here at the bottom. Okay, got it. Let's get going."

Gates closed out the laptop connection, making sure to clear their browser history—didn't want to leave any trace of their presence here—and they left the booth.

Only to find two of the bar's three customers standing in their way.

One came slightly more than waist high to Jeanne, vaguely humanoid but with feline features and covered in orange fur. A K'ttn. It hissed in displeasure at Gates.

The other towered over all of them, a Zebra-striped Loper: four slim legs like bendy straws stretching up to a disproportionately small oval body with a crane-like neck and anteater sort of head. Good for sucking up those high tree-dwelling bug-slugs on its home world, and running away from several really fast predators they had there.

The third of the bar's customers sat by itself some distance away, a small hunched creature, evidently disinterested in anything other than its drink and its own troubles.

The cat-man (as Jeanne thought of him) pointed a furry paw, or hand, or whatever, at the rolled-up shadow cloak she carried. In a deceptively quiet voice it said, "That interesting piece of cloth."

Galactic Trade Standard, but a bit more sophisticated than the robo bartender's. "Nothing special," she responded. "Excuse us, please." She started forward again.

The two aliens moved to block her path. "Perhaps," the K'ttn said softly, "we make deal. I might be in market for such cloth."

"Sorry, not selling. Now let us pass."

That furry paw extended tentatively. "Catches my eye. Make you fair price."

Jeanne keyed her private comm. "Gates, I don't like this."

Gates gave a low throaty growl.

The K'ttn hissed again and took a step back. "Control your pet!"

"He controls himself. And no means no. We're done now."

The two aliens exchanged looks. From the Loper's body over their heads a pair of grasping appendages previously hidden by its stripes unfolded.

Meanwhile the cat-man's paw-hands flared, exposing a mean set of claws. "I know that is more than just piece of cloth. I *will* have it!"

"Oh oh," Jeanne said to Gates. "Looks like we're getting physical!"

No time to activate her rejuvenation or even her senssuit, as the Loper reached down surprisingly quickly and grabbed her arms. At the same time the cat-man pounced in to make a swipe for the cloak.

Gates leaped into action, biting down on the cat arm and throwing both of them backward in a ball of squabbling fur, loud shrieks and growls, and knocking over a table and chairs in the process, scrapping like—well, like cats and dogs.

Jeanne couldn't help him since she had her hands full. Or rather, she *was* the handful: the Loper had picked her off the floor and began shaking her violently. She struggled against its grip while trying to keep hold of the shadow cloak.

Out of the corner of her eye she saw the robo barkeep detach itself from its rail, rise up on its arms and leap over the bar. It extended a pair of folding steel legs from its undercarriage and sped toward them in a blur.

She wasn't sure exactly what happened next, except she felt the Loper jerk as if hit and an electric current shoot through her—fortunately buffered by her suit even in its de-activated state. Released from the Loper's grip she fell to the floor. The alien toppled the other way, stunned—it must have absorbed most of the voltage. The robo bartender turned and propelled itself toward the other two combatants.

"Gates, evade!" she called out.

Gates obediently leaped away from his opponent just as the robo bartender-turned-bouncer clamped a mechanical hand on the K'ttn's leg. With a piercing cat screech orange fur shot erect and its limbs quivered involuntarily.

Jeanne scrambled to her feet and unfurled the shadow cloak. "Gates, here boy!"

Gates bounded over, Jeanne whirled the garment to cover both of them, found the activator switch sewn into the center and flicked it on. She drew both of them off to one side next to the line of curtained booths. "Quiet boy! Stay. Don't move."

She tried to still her breathing. From inside, the cloak gave no hindrance to external vision, and they could clearly see the two aliens lying unconscious on the floor with the robo bartender-bouncer standing over them on its stilt-legs. Jeanne began to see now why it had so many scars and dings on its metal casing. Its head rotated as it searched the room for more objectionable behavior. Those glowing yellow visual sensors passed over them, paused, tracked back for a heart-stopping moment, then continued on.

Jeanne gave a silent sigh and looked down at her companion. But the cloak's light-bending environment played tricks in here and she couldn't see much beyond her own nose. "Are you injured?" she whispered—needlessly since they were on their private comms.

"Minor scratches. Nothing a few good tongue licks won't heal."

"Then we move together, slowly toward the exit."

She knew the cloak's metasurface would show visual distortions if they moved too quickly or abruptly. Active camouflage technology was good, but not perfect. So inch by steady inch, like walking while balancing a plate on your head, and maybe an egg on the plate.

The metal guardian began making a slow tour of the room. It stopped momentarily by the third of the bar's customers who had remained completely indifferent this entire time, still hunched at its table nursing whatever consciousness-altering concoction its biology preferred. It lifted its drink to the robot in a listless toast.

As they neared the front entrance Gates said, "What do we do if the door's locked?"

"From the inside? I'm guessing they still have to obey fire

code regulations even in this part of town."

"You're *guessing?*"

"We're about to find out. Get ready to run when I push on the exit handle."

Only a few steps to go. The robo bouncer had circled back by now and progressed halfway down the room, coming toward them.

Gates must have gotten a little over-anxious. He accidentally stepped on the hem of the cloak. It shifted sharply.

The robot's eyes snapped around to fix directly on them.

"It's seen us!" Jeanne cried. "Go!"

They hit the door just as the robot zoomed up behind them. But the latch yielded, and with a burst of speed they were through and onto the street before those electrified hands could touch them.

The robot halted at the threshold, glared at them coldly, then withdrew inside and slammed the door.

"That metallic menace kind of has a split personality, wouldn't you say?" Gates remarked.

"Well, you can't really blame him, can you, tasked as he is with managing that place."

"Him?"

"Or her. Or it. Whatever robots are." Jeanne switched off the cloak and rolled it up again—hastily and discretely so as not to attract anyone else who might be in the mood to relieve them of such a desirable item. She did a quick check of the few sketchy pedestrians in the area, decided it best not to linger. "Let's get moving. We've lost time that we'll have to make up. You're sure you're all right?"

Gates gave a doggie snort. "No furry-faced fake feline is going to get the better of me!"

"That's my fearless guard dog. Now if I've got my

directions right we go that way." She pointed up an intersecting street toward the many shiny high-rise structures in the heart of downtown, visible in the distance over the plain and homely roof tops and humble buildings of the old quarter.

As they set off, still keeping as much as possible out of view of any surveillance devices, Gates said, "You know, our dust-up with that cat guy has me wondering. When the Agency did my genetic enhancements why couldn't they have given me hands like he has?"

Jeanne looked surprised. "Jealous, Gates? Poor boy! I suppose it would be nice. But then you couldn't pass for an ordinary dog. And since you're a super-secret augmented spy canine that's not even supposed to exist, they couldn't do that. Sorry, partner. Just remember that I appreciate all your many other gifts. And that we're best friends no matter what."

Gates wagged his tail.

"It is curious, though," Jeanne mused, "how our two friendly thieves back there knew about this cloak. When turned off it looks like any other piece of cloth. At least to me."

"Me too. Maybe it's those cat eyes. Might have special vision—you know, like how cats can see in the dark." Gates shivered as if he considered the idea so foreign to him as to be magic.

"Maybe. Or maybe he's already familiar with the technology, worked with it before and can recognize it where the untrained person can't. In any case, this should be a reminder that we can't take anything for granted or assume anything, now that we're out here on our own. An important lesson." She shaded her eyes against the afternoon sun. "You know, those downtown buildings don't look any closer. We'd better pick up the pace, or find a faster way to travel."

"No air cabs around this part of town. Not even a robo cycle. But we'll enter the outskirts of the main city in a few more blocks. We should find something then."

"It better be something inexpensive."

Gates went into hunt mode. Shortly he spotted something far up the street. "You mean like that?"

"What? Oh...is that what I think it is?"

They hurried forward the few intervening blocks. Just this side of the unofficial boundary between the old quarter and the city proper a flitty-flyer rested at the curb on its four curved landing legs. The little ultra-light conveyance must be waiting for a fare, or have just dropped one off. A bit unusual, maybe, outside of the more lucrative commercial areas, but probably not unheard of.

As they drew near they could see why: The hollow insect-like body bore scrapes and patches and dubious repairs, and the translucent bee wings looked time-worn and about as air-worthy as a kite that's been through a hurricane.

They slowed. "I don't think this is such a good idea," Jeanne said out loud. "That thing won't even get off the ground."

"Who says!" a light but confident voice demanded in English.

They turned. From the shaded doorway of a decrepit brick building a small garden gnome stepped out—at least that's how Jeanne thought of it. She knew the pilots of flitty-flyers had to be small and lightweight if they were going to carry passengers, and this planet's indigenous species of "forest fairies" as they were called by humans made them the natural choice. (Or maybe it was forest "ferries," since that's what they did: ferry people around.)

"You speak English?" she said.

The gnome—a female from form and uncannily human-like facial features topped by tightly-braided brown-and-gold-dappled hair—put her tiny hands on the hips of her belted flight jacket. "Well I should think that's obvious, seeing as how you're hearing it. Sometimes I think you humans are the most obtuse creatures in the universe, have to have everything explained to you. Yes, those of us who work for human companies in human cities learn human languages. Big surprise. Now that that's out of the way, you insulted my ship. I expect an apology. Well? What do you have to say?"

"Uh...sorry if I offended you. Or your ship. But I really do question it's safety."

"Ha! Why, I'll have you know this little honey is safe as a summer sprinkle on a flower bed. She'll fly rings around any other flyer in the city! 'Long as I'm the pilot, that is. I'll get you where you want to go, don't doubt it." She stood firm and stared at them with fierce eyes.

Jeanne couldn't help but smile inwardly at the creature's moxie. She still had serious doubts about the flyer, though. She spoke on her private comm. "Gates, do you have an opinion?"

Gates had been sniffing around the fuselage, up on his hind legs peering through the clear nose canopy. "Hard to tell. The mechanics and instrumentation seem sound. Damage and repairs appear mostly superficial, the key word being 'appear.' I suspect it *will* fly, but how well I won't put dog treats—or money—on."

Jeanne looked over at the soaring city buildings, still a good ways off, then back at the dilapidated flyer. "There's no way we'll make the consulate on time by foot. Then again, we might not make it all in this thing."

The gnome-slash-forest fairy meanwhile had grown

impatient, unaware of their unspoken conversation. "Made up your mind yet? Or are you going to stand there all day looking dazed?"

"Uh, just considering our options. We're trying to get to the Spraang consulate. It's over near—"

"I know where it is! I've been ferrying fares around this city since humans put up their first shanty shack here. I know more places in this over-grown ant hill than all the places on all the planets you've ever been to!"

Jeanne recalled her pre-arrival briefing about this world, and the extremely long lifespans these gnomes (sorry, forest fairies) were alleged to have. "It's just that we need to get there by 5:00 pm...."

"5:00 pm! Then no time to dawdle. We have to get cracking!" The little creature stepped around behind Jeanne and began pushing her from the rear (literally the rear, though where those tiny hands landed on her is not a subject for discussion).

But it seemed the decision had been made. The bubble canopy rolled up and back and the little gnome boosted her (with considerable and not very effective effort) into one of the two front seats. Gates hopped in next to her. Safety harnesses engineered to accommodate a variety of species auto-adjusted to their shapes, although Gates had a little trouble getting his to let him sit up straight.

The gnome skittered into the pilot perch above and behind them both. "Name's Trix," she offered as she settled into her harness and began flipping switches. "That's a human nickname, o' course. My real name you couldn't pronounce." She slipped her hands into the two omni-controllers on the armrests and the craft came alive, rocked slightly forward as the wings extended to the sides.

"Fun fact," she continued as the wings began sweeping

forward and backward, speeding up briskly and becoming nearly a blur, their sound a deep humming or buzzing even once the canopy slid closed. "These flyers are actually modeled on a little creature on your human world of Earth. Bumble bees."

With a sway the vehicle lifted lightly off the ground. Jeanne held on with barely-concealed insecurity as they gained altitude, angling over the tops of nearby buildings toward the city center. Gates, however, seemed unperturbed for the most part.

The pilot prattled on over the thrumming of the wings. "For a long time your human scientists thought bumble bees shouldn't be able to fly, according to the laws of aerodynamics. Their wings aren't big enough or strong enough, not like a bird's. Not until super-slow-mo video showed them that bees don't actually flap their wings like a bird, they hold their wing surfaces vertical and *scull* them back and forth! Yup. So fast that they buzz. That's why bees—and these flyers—can hover in place and flit around where no other aircraft can. Ha! Score one for good-ol' nature."

They'd begun passing above the outskirts of the main metro area now, still climbing. Despite Trix's extolling the merits of her flying machine, Jeanne couldn't help feeling queasy looking down through the bubble canopy only inches from her face at the empty space growing between her and the now well-maintained and laid-out cityscape below. She tried to focus her attention forward, on the impressive architecture of Lusteer's city center rising before them and getting rapidly closer. But other flyers and increasingly dense aircar traffic kept diverting her attention—and her nerves.

"Not much of a talker, are you?" Trix commented.

Jeanne didn't get a chance to answer as another flitty-flyer zipped by close in front and above them. She flinched.

Trix compensated smoothly for the slight air disturbance. "I get the sense you've never flown in one of these before. Don't worry, even if you weren't in the experienced and exceptionally capable hands of the best pilot on the planet, these things have proximity detectors and computer control safeties that prevent collisions. We're safer up here than anywhere down there in that lunatic playpen, that I can tell you! Why I could close my eyes and take a nap—"

"Please don't!"

"Oh, I won't. I'm as alert a pilot as you'll find, believe me. Some of these other pilots, though—oof! I could tell you stories. Still, our overall industry safety record is pretty darn clean, all things considered. I'm just saying...hang on, we're approaching the consulate. You want the roof or the ground loading loop?"

They were swinging in high between two massive metal-and-glass spires among a dozen other gleaming spires. A multiplicity of smaller but no-less splendid domes and pyramids and twisting arches artfully speckled the ground below, while air traffic of all kinds whizzed in orderly chaos all around.

Jeanne ventured a look down into the canyon-like depths at the multi-level walkways and countless dot-sized galactic citizens going about their affairs. "Uh, ground loop will do. But set us on the outer landing rim, away from the entrance."

"Ground floor it is." She put the flyer into a nose dive, sending Jeanne's stomach careening into her throat. Other air vehicles screamed by perilously close, and several times they dodged and zagged to avoid certain death.

Jeanne hung on as the concrete landing pad rushed up at

them way too fast, until at the last second Trix pulled out of the dive with a gee-force Jeanne was sure the tiny craft couldn't tolerate. They decelerated rapidly to just a few feet off the pavement, hovered, and touched down gently.

Trix throttled down her engines. "We have arrived at your destination. VIP service all the way! And on time, too—three minutes early in fact. That'll be fifteen Galactic bucks. How do you want to pay?"

Their safety harnesses released. Jeanne swallowed, then untensed and counted out the required coinage, figuring in her head their remaining reserves. At this rate their meager funds wouldn't last much longer.

"Cash?" Trix scrutinized her two passengers skeptically as she deposited the payment in her vehicle's strongbox, automatically unlocking and retracting the nose canopy to allow exit. "Hmm. Look, maybe it's none of my business, but I've been doing this long enough to know when someone's in trouble or on the run, and you have all the classic signs."

Jeanne stiffened. So did Gates.

Trix stuck out a palm. "Oh, don't get jumpy, I'm not going to rat you out or anything. Goodness knows, I've been in a tough spot a couple of times myself. What I'm saying is...I'm a pretty good judge of character, and I don't think you're a bad person. Just someone in a jam."

"Is it that obvious?"

"Only to a super keen observer like me. I don't know who or what you're running from, but—maybe I'm just a sucker for an underdog or a sap with a big heart—but if you need my services again or my vast and unmatched expertise, I might be able to make myself available. Heck, for an animal lover with such a fine mutual bond with their little buddy there like you obviously have, I'll even cut my usual fee in half. Don't tell anybody I said that! You can zing me on any of the social platforms. Trix-One-Oh-Oh-Two-Nine, that's my handle."

"Uh, I don't think that will be necessary. But thanks."

"Well, the offer's there, anyway. Better give me your name, though, just in case."

"Jeanne."

"All right, Jeanne. Good luck to you. And your cute little sidekick, too!"

They climbed out. Trix called after them, "Remember my handle!" Then she fed power to her flyer and with a thrumming buzz flitted up and away.

* * * *

They faced the Spraang consulate, a rather modest six-story dome amongst all these other imposing edifices, but still aesthetically lovely, its rose-pink surface glowing with a soft inner light here in the shadows of its taller cousins. Jeanne motioned Gates toward a nearby covered walkway. "Let's get out of sight. Roingroing should be leaving any minute."

"You think you can pick him out from all these other Spraangs?"

He had a point. This being the Spraang's official center of activity on this world, any number of pinkish dodge-ball shapes came and went at their leisure, shooting out pseudopods and bouncing or rolling along on whatever business mattered to Dodge-balls.

"I'm not going to. You are."

"Me?" Gates gave a quizzical look.

"You've met him. You got his scent, didn't you?"

"Oh! Sometimes I forget I'm a dog."

"I'm guessing each Spraang has a unique smell, just like humans do, right?"

"Yes, and it's even more pronounced since small amounts

of their gases leak out constantly."

"So get downwind of the entrance, maybe behind one of those potted red bushes along the approach walkway. Not too close, we don't want security chasing after you as a stray. I'll stay here in the shadows until you signal me."

Gates gave a soft woof of consent and galloped off.

They didn't have long to wait. At precisely 5:00 pm several pinkish dodge-ball shapes exited the consulate, heading for a line of air and ground taxis parked around the edge of the loading loop.

Gates sniffed the breeze, seeking a telltale odor. "Got him!" He went into pointer position.

"Great. Do you think you can cut him off? Separate him from the others?"

Gates dashed out to meet the unsuspecting bureaucrat, began running around in front of him and barking.

The distraction made Roingroing stop while the other Spraang moved on without him, leaving him momentarily alone.

"That's enough," Jeanne said to Gates. "Pull his attention around toward me." When he did so she leaned into the open and gave a "Pssst!"

The Spraang being air bags who made squeaks, whistles and hisses themselves, they were especially sensitive to such sounds. Roingroing oriented his sensors in her direction—at least she assumed he did since no one knew just where Spraang had their sensors on those featureless pink spheres. She leaned further out and gestured for him to come to her.

He bounced his way over. "Ambasssador Jeanne! What isss thisss about?"

In a hushed voice she said, "Sorry to disturb your evening routine, but something urgent has come up. Highest priority. Is there somewhere private we can talk? Away from prying ears—er, I mean away from acoustic tympanic membranes? Somewhere *ultra* private and ultra secure."

Roingroing quickly processed this unexpected and most seriously-phrased request. But being the literal-minded species he was he accepted her words at face value. "Come thisss way." He bounced off on a side path leading around the side of the consulate, not so fast that Jeanne's human legs couldn't keep up. Gates trotted behind, keeping an eye out for threats, and an ear and nose too.

The Spraang sub-attaché led them to a high-fenced courtyard in back, where an extensive garden of exotic plants and flowers with a predominantly red-and-pink color pallet, doubtless imported from his home world, sprawled in a broad crescent behind the consulate dome. In the middle of the garden a miniature dome mimicking its bigger parent nestled amongst the alien flora and meandering paths. Roingroing stopped beside this, extruded a pseudopod and activated a sliding door in its side.

They entered into an igloo-like environment maybe five or six meters across, with wine-red cushions covering the floor. Little serving tables made from some dark-grained wood projected at intervals from around the walls, and a central basin of reddish liquid shimmered in raised polished rock a few inches above the floor. Small lights of some type inside the liquid illuminated the interior with a diffuse crimson ambience. The lights seemed to crawl slowly around the basin of their own accord—bioluminescent creatures maybe?

Roingroing sealed the door and rolled onto a cushion. "Thisss isss a meditatsssion sssanctuary. We come here for sssolitude and introsssspection. It isss, asss you sssay, ultra private and ultra sssecure."

Jeanne felt a release of heaviness—for the first time in

awhile now. "You're sure no one can listen in here?"

"I'm sssure. There are no electronicsss or other meansss of outssside connectsssion. And the wallsss are ssspecially consssstructed for ssseclusion and privasssy."

"Very well." She lowered herself cross-legged onto the cushion-floor. "First off, have you heard any reports or news about me today, or about the Goodwill Council?"

"Reportsss? No. The Councsssil hasss been ssstrangely sssilent thisss afternoon. No communicationsss in or out—although that in itssself isss mysssstifying, I confesss."

Jeanne grew solemn. "Roingroing, I'm going to trust you with some of the most important—and dangerous—information I've ever run across. I do so because I need your help. My life, all our lives, the lives of everyone in our galaxy, are in the gravest possible danger!"

Roingroing's reply sounded carefully measured. "Thisss isss a ssseriousss ssstatement. I asssume you have ssstrong evidencssse to sssupport these allegationsss?"

"Very strong. At least I think so. I'm hoping you'll agree. But...maybe it's best just to show you." On her private comm she said, "Gates, get ready to project a holo of that collapsing galaxy video. Include the intelligence verification code and data analysis readout."

"Are you sure that's a good idea?" Gates returned. "He's going to wonder how we came by that kind of intelligence."

"Just get it ready." Out loud she said to Roingroing, "You remember how shocked I was earlier today from what I learned during my meeting with the Gu'gundreans?"

"Yesss. Well, they do converssse with electrisssity."

Curse his literalness. "I mean psychologically shocked. Upset. Startled."

"Ah. The notoriousss human inexactnesss. It isss difficult for my ssspeciesss to make sssensse of such sssloppy—I mean imprecissse—double meaningsss."

"Yeah, I'll try to be more careful. Well the Gu'gundreans showed me something unimaginably terrible. Something I didn't believe at first, or didn't want to believe. But it confirmed another piece of upsetting intelligence I'd already received from...let's just say reliable sources I work with outside my ambassadorial duties when I need special information not available through normal channels."

"A ssside hussstle?"

"Something like that." She signaled Gates: "Now."

From Gates's collar a holo image projected into the air, showing the astonishingly impossible time-lapsed galaxy disappearance she'd seen only hours earlier. At the bottom an Agency 3-D un-hackable intelligence code signature and qubit-encrypted verification stamp glowed in scarlet Galactic Standard letters, along with the classification warning "Way Way WAY Above Top Secret!"

Roingroing watched the video to the end, read the attached summary analysis.

"Well?" Jeanne prompted.

"I won't asssk how you came by thessse assstounding imagesss. They are disssturbing to sssay the leassst. However, the embedded sssecurity code isss indisssputable, ssso I can't doubt the authentisssity—or the abysssmal conclusssion." He pondered. Finally he said, "The analyssisss sssuggessstsss thisss wasss a deliberate act, yet it doesss not tell usss who isss ressssponsssible."

"That's where the Gu'gundreans come in. And from there I can fill in the rest." She then explained what the Gu'gundreans had showed her, that it was some power bloc within the Goodwill Council itself behind this nefarious conspiracy to threaten and terrorize all other galaxies, how this cabal had tried to sabotage her meeting with the

Gu'gundreans, then when that didn't work they sent an assassin after her, from whom they'd intercepted a direct comm to the Big Boss at the head of it all: Senior Goodwill Councilor Leonore Squag herself.

To confirm that mind-boggling last part Jeanne had Gates play his recording of the intercepted comm squirt with all its metadata.

Roingroing shuddered, a curious phenomenon for a gas bag. "I sssuppossse I am, as you sssay, ssshocked by thessse revelationsss."

"It's a lot to take in."

Roingroing sat silent a long time. But the thing about Spraang is, they didn't need much convincing. They saw something, they believed it. Literally.

He said, "These thingsss you've ssshowed me require a level of confidential intelligencsse a ssstandard ambasssador ssshould have no accesss to, and a technical capability you ssshould not posssesss. I'm alssso curiousss how it isss that your dog isss the one sssupplying all the recordingsss and technical detailsss."

Jeanne stayed expressionless.

Roingroing went on, "I begin to sssusssspect there isss more to you than you disssclose. But in view of the high sssecurity clearancsse, perhapsss I ssshouldn't asssk. You sssaid you needed my help."

Jeanne gave an inward sigh. She'd been unsure how he'd respond. "We have to expose the plot, get this information to those who can take action to stop it. You have connections, here and off world. We need trusted people in government—no wait, that's an oxymoron. Well, in intelligence and law enforcement services then. You must know some non-human agencies that won't be intimidated by the Council, and that have at least some dedication to the truth. Maybe you can get your own consulate to take notice, start something going, liaise with other worlds. I realize that will subject you to unwelcome scrutiny and skepticism, but you're the only one who can do it."

Roingroing trembled. "No, that'sss too much! You ssseem to think I have more sssway than I do. I am only a sssub-attaché!"

"Yet you're what we've got. If we're going to save the galaxy, we need *you* to help us make that happen."

Roingroing began rocking nervously, letting out a distraught steady hiss.

Jeanne hoped she hadn't broken him—just deflated him a little.

Chapter 3

Roingroing's stress-rocking became an unsteady precession around his vertical axis. "You've ssstuck me in an imposssible posssition!"

For several minutes they'd tried all they could think of to calm him down, but he seemed agitated beyond soothing.

"Look," Jeanne said. "You're not alone. You've got us, and once we convince a few others we're bound to have all kinds of backup and support. The Gu'gundreans are already on our side. They're the ones who first discovered the Goodwill Council's involvement. I'm sure they'd be more than happy to tell their story, and even testify in galactic high court."

Roingroing stopped rocking. "The Gu'gundreansss! If what you've sssaid isss true, their delegation isss at risssk! They cannot leave their ssswimming pool. If the counsssil sssendsss more asssasssinsss...."

"I know." This problem had been nagging at Jeanne, too, yet she didn't have a solution. "They're sitting ducks."

"Ducksss? You ssseem confusssed. They are not ducksss."

"It's another sloppy human impreciSion—a figure of speech. It means they're defenseless and can't protect themselves."

"That isss true. It would be sssimple enough to neutralizzze the alkalinity of their pool'sss mucousss sssolution with a sssizeable quantity of sssome assscidic sssubstance. None would sssurvive."

"So how do we protect them? Without getting ourselves

killed. You can bet the Council will have someone waiting for me if I try to go back into the hotel. You might be able to get close, but they're going to need round-the-clock protection, and the two of us alone aren't enough...."

Roingroing did the Spraang counterpart of sitting upright. "A sssceremony!"

"Huh? This is no time for formal etiquette! We need action."

"Action, yesss." He rotated while he thought, then anchored himself with pseudopods. "A ssscelebration, a big one, right at poolssside. I propossse we sssurround the Gu'gundreansss with lotsss of diplomatsss and sssecretariesss, and nonsssstop banquetsss and ssspeechesss and awardsss. You humansss call it pomp and ssscircumstancsse. We'll make it lassst for daysss, weeksss if necesssary. That'sss sssomething I'm ssskilled at, and can ssset up through my consssulate."

Jeanne blinked. "Roingroing, you may have something there! We can have velvet rope barriers with alarms and hand-picked security to keep everyone away from the pool— for their own safety, of course. No assassin or saboteur could get close. Splendid idea, Roingroing! I believe it will work. Let's get started." She rose to her feet, then stopped. "Uh, we'd better install some serious ventilation first thing, though."

* * * *

They set about putting their plan into motion: filing city permits and getting consulate approval and hotel authorization (with a rush contractor deal for a super-ventilation modification) and pulling together catering and decorating services and sending out priority notices and invitations to the many notables and eminent personages already present in this world's capitol city of Lusteer, and more offworld, and handling all the other logistical and practical rigmarole required to organize such a major function.

At the same time Roingroing quietly and clandestinely began feeling out a few trusted contacts he thought might help with their other more secret objective, both within the Spraang consulate and outside it, setting a preliminary foundation for leaking the disquieting information Ambassador Jeanne had brought him, hopefully to where it might do the most good. But bureaucratic machinery turns ponderously, with great inertia and resistance to anything that doesn't conform to routine or that attempts to circumvent normal channels. Roingroing found the going frustratingly slow and arduous.

Meanwhile Jeanne and Gates took up temporary residence in one of the Spraang consulate's ancillary bungalows designed to house visitors, keeping well hidden while trying to help out with event planning as best they could—by routing communiqués and memos, coordinating purchase orders and schedules and inevitable conflicts, all without cyber-neural comms or even old-fashioned video or any other way of divulging their identities.

But however haphazardly, the celebration—or as Gates called it, the bigwig shindig—got underway, thrown together in record time and hyped publicly as the VIP party not to be missed. Dignitaries from many planets and governments and species came to pay their respects, make welcoming speeches, do photo ops, or just put in a pompous and showy public appearance. The Gu'gundreans would pop their heads (or the goo-being equivalent) up now and then to look over the spectacle. Translators stationed at booths on the pool corners did their limited best to convey attendees' sentiments both ways.

News and social media covered the big to-do with continual commentary as the social extravaganza of the year. Festivities quickly overflowed to fill adjacent hallways and conference rooms and ballrooms, with multitudes of A-listers and B-listers coming and going at all hours (and even C and D and E listers, and on down the alphabet for species who used alphabets). It became a self-sustaining phenomenon—no matter that most of those present quickly forgot its intended purpose to honor the Gu'gundreans. And of course the hotel happily raked in windfall profits.

But all-in-all the gala atmosphere did its job: no nasty dark-ops types could get through the blockade of pretentious pageantry, ostentatious officials and fawning functionaries.

Roingroing himself, given his leading role in bringing the affair about, found his standing instantly elevated among his fellows at the consulate, and even with diplomats from other embassies—a boost in status he didn't find at all displeasing.

That notoriety came with both good and bad aspects, however. Channels of communication now opened for him that had been unavailable before, as well as unexpected offers of friendship, or what passed for it in the political realm. On the negative side his newfound prominence made him more conspicuously visible—to both wanted and very *unwanted* attention. And that latter prospect brought him a new and highly *unpleasant* anxiety.

From time to time Jeanne and Gates would meet with him secretly in the Spraang meditation dome behind the consulate to discuss how things were going. Jeanne found the muted bioluminescent lighting and reddish atmosphere calming after the stress of Roingroing's hectic diplomatic world and the ever-present threat from the Council hanging over their heads.

Unfortunately, Roingroing had little to report. After a few meetings he finally had to concede dismally that the contacts he'd thought promising were fast drying up (Jeanne added that metaphor, Roingroing himself would never use anything so non-literal). It seems both his old contacts and new "friendships" had started getting serious pressure from the Council to back off, to not get involved in helping him. And most of them, being good well-entrenched bureaucrats and not wanting to incur the formidable ire of the Council of Goodwill, complied.

"I suppose I should have expected that," Jeanne grumbled gloomily. "Leonore Squag and her Council cronies no doubt have cyber spy bots trolling all communication lines for any hint of chatter regarding them—or me. Especially official communication lines like you're using from your consulate."

Roingroing squeaked. "But that'sss illegal! By galactic covenantsss, no governmentsss or agenssscies can lisssten in on csssitizen communicationsss!"

"You think a little thing like galactic law is going to deter self-serving types like these? I could show you plenty of examp...well, that's a matter for another discussion."

"In that cassse, my attemptsss to elissscit aid from offworld sssourcesss may have ssserved only to expossse usss!"

"Unfortunately, yes. You're on the Council's radar now—sorry, I mean they've connected you with me, so we're both their targets now."

Roingroing began rocking and letting out an agitated hiss again.

"Don't give up hope yet. You've got some protection from your position with the consulate. You're too much in the public eye for them to act overtly against you, especially right now with the success of our 'pool party.' The Council is still operating in secret, so they don't dare take out someone so prominent as you've become."

Roingroing seemed slightly mollified, though unsure of her wording. "Take out?"

"Uh, let's not go into that metaphor. What I'm saying is Leonore's faction of the Council hasn't made any public threats or demands like we thought they would, so I'm thinking they're only planning on doing so with specific government leaders. It's looking now like they want to keep the general public blissfully ignorant while they take control of everything behind the scenes—a massive, silent power grab, the biggest one in the history of the universe!" She paused. "But it also means they're not going to do anything to risk their ultimate objective, certainly not anything so clumsily open as assassinating one minor sub-attaché."

"Asssasssinating!" Roingroing's entire membrane surface shivered.

"Oh, I'd give that a pretty low probability. You'll just have to be a little more careful from now on, pay more attention to where you go and how exposed you are, and not leave the consulate grounds unless absolutely necessary. As long as we stay here we're legally on sovereign foreign soil and can't be touched."

Gates, who had remained silent for this whole exchange, spoke now on Jeanne's personal comm: "I hate to point this out, but they could send a secret assassin like they did with us. Keep everything cloak-and-dagger."

Jeanne switched to her private circuit. "Let's not give Roingroing anything else to worry about."

"If you say so. It just seems to me that if they know he's been helping us, and can get at him, then they can get at us, too."

"Yeah, that thought hadn't escaped me. All right, new

plan: we go on the offensive." To Roingroing she said, "So if we can't count on help from outside agencies or governments, which is what you're telling me, then we have only one alternative: It's up to us to find out where they have the device planted and how it's triggered."

"Usss? Are you ssseriousss?"

"We don't have much choice. Did you learn anything at all from your inquiries off-world?"

"Disssappointingly little. Only that Sssenior Counsssilor Leonore Sssquag isss arriving to finisssh the negotiationsss with the Gu'gundreanss in perssson, sssince you botched the job yoursssself. Thossse are her wordsss."

"In person? That's a twist. Wonder what for? Aside from her officially stated reason. It's certainly not to help the Gu'gundreans, we can be sure of that. If anything it's the opposite—besides whatever her bigger purpose might be."

"Thossse are sssolid asssumptionsss."

"They'll have her heavily guarded, surrounded by legions of sycophants and toadies." (Actual toads, or toad-humanoids: a race of muscular toad people who hire out as warrior mercenaries). "She'll be impossible to get to."

"Then we ssseem to be, asss you humansss sssay, back to sssquare one."

"Huh, is that a metaphor? Good for you, Roingroing! You got that one right. Except the difference now is this new development puts the focus of danger right in our laps."

"And ssshe hasss consssiderably more power than usss."

"True. Then again, that power makes her overconfident, more prone to making mistakes. Hmm. Give me a minute to think." She went private again. "Gates, I'm getting an idea. Do you think you can sneak into the hotel through some back way?"

"Like the kitchen?" Gates's tail wagged in anticipation.

"No time to be thinking of treats! I'm talking infiltration, a covert mission."

"I can probably get into their system of service elevators. But once on any given floor I'll have to use the regular hallways like anyone else."

"That'll have to do. I need you to get back to our hotel room and retrieve my goo suit."

"Oh?"

"If Leonore is going to meet with the Gu'gundreans herself, I want to be there when she does, if only to make sure the Gu'gundreans stay safe. And maybe to find out a little about what she's up to."

"That could be risky. What's your plan?"

"Still working on that. I figure she'll have to shut down the main ceremonial hoopla around the swimming pool for her meeting—and she has the Council's clout to do it. But there'll still be guards and media cameras and lots of public attention all over the place. So she won't dare do anything to show her true hand. But first things first. I need my goo suit."

Roingroing broke in, "You two ssstare at each other ssstrangely. It'sss almossst asss if I'm misssing sssomething going on between you."

Jeanne stirred. "Just thinking. We've...I mean I've got a plan now, or at least the beginning of one. When is Leonore Squag scheduled to meet with the Gu'gundreans? I need an exact itinerary."

"Are you going to tell me thisss plan?"

"I will, but let's see how this first part goes. And for that, we need you to get us a ride."

* * * *

Gates left Jeanne in the ground taxi two blocks from the hotel and stole up to a rear receiving entrance, one of several loading docks. This particular entrance led to a store room near one of the sixteen five-star kitchens the hotel boasted. Gates salivated at rich aromas of sauces and meats and stews—or their synthetic substitutes anyway. Also at plenty of rotting garbage from dumpsters in the loading area parking lot.

He licked his chops and moved closer. Only three shipping containers had been set down by sky transports at the moment, backed up to loading doors in the receiving area. Gates kept clear of them and slunk around toward the kitchen entrance on his side of the parking lot.

Clear plastic strips hung in each loading doorway, a lightweight barrier separating the outside world from inside—easy to push through. Gates slipped quickly in and angled off to take cover behind a stack of boxes and crates. From some distance away workers' voices drifted to him, but the immediate way seemed clear. He padded forward, heading toward a two-way swinging door evidently used by robot forklifts and automated pallet jacks. He listened at the threshold, then nudged the door open enough to let him through.

A food staging area greeted him on the other side, with walk-in freezers along one wall and rows of work tables and shelves crowding the rest. Much of the unboxing and shelf-filling and such was mechanized, but a number of live scullery personnel—mostly a small imp-like scavenger species that didn't mind scut work—idly tended to the lesser details, or the messier ones. Gates took advantage of a passing robo-cart, hid behind it as it rolled toward access to the kitchen itself at the far end of the room.

He dropped off once inside while the cart joined a queue of similar carts lined up for off-loading of raw foodstuffs. Much swankier in here: more elaborate automation, fancy ovens and ranges and steaming cookery pouring out a hodgepodge of tasty smells. But also a few live cooks and chefs from different worlds and culinary traditions. Gates kept low and tried to sneak past the multiple meal-prep islands in the center.

He got about halfway when a yell told him someone had spotted him. He snatched a tempting morsel of chicken (or something) from the edge of a countertop and took off running. He made it to the door to the dining area and hit it just as a robo bus boy came through the other way, sending it and its tray of unbreakable china flying with a loud clatter and startling a human waitress who similarly went flying with an even louder squeal. He bounded across the ritzy dining hall between astonished patrons, brushing tablecloths and hearing the clatter of more falling dinnerware, not looking back to see what other havoc he might have caused.

Once out of the dining room he veered sharply, located a side corridor used for maintenance and scrambled down it— he knew they had one of these next to each of their big venue rooms. It would have a service elevator at the end. He also knew the elevators had security locks that would have to be bypassed. Fortunately his classified Agency spy software and near-field cyber-electronics made such tasks relative puppy's play.

He finished his "chicken" treat enroute to the elevator and examined the security lock. No surprises, just a basic multi-scanner designed to suit different species' anatomies: retinal scan, face recognition, thumb or palm or paw print, voice/sonic pattern match, DNA signature, a gas-scent molecular analyzer (probably for the Spraang, Gates could appreciate that one), and a couple of others he didn't know.

His cyber-neural implants connected wirelessly with the

lock and decrypted it in short order. The elevator opened. He entered and scrolled the menu to select the nine-hundred-twentieth floor. As a precaution he had his software disable any calls for stops on other floors. Best to make this an express trip.

Nine hundred twenty floors is a long ride up, even in an elevator that zipped along on frictionless magnetic guide rails rather than cables and wheel tracks. Gates waited nervously until the doors opened, hoping he wouldn't encounter any of the custodial crew, even though most of the hotel's grunt work was done by robots—live waitresses and maitre de's and such being really just a novelty for the amusement of affluent guests who patronized the restaurants and gift shops and lobby areas.

He'd guessed right. The elevator opened onto another service corridor where a roundish blue room-service bot, its multiple arms and cleaning devices retracted, rolled in next to him without so much as a glance his way. He trotted out and down the corridor.

He halted at the end and peeked around the corner. A long orange-carpeted hallway stretched into the distance, lined with platinum-hued room doors and elegant seashell lighting sconces. And standing right in front of their former room: two burly and none-too-friendly-looking guards in black uniforms with really ugly faces. Those mercenary toad guys!

He drew back. An unexpected obstacle.

Could he get past them? Not much chance without a fight, and the odds weren't in his favor. Distract them away from their post? Unlikely from what he knew of born-and-bred military types. He seemed to be stuck.

He had to report this to Jeanne—and risk someone intercepting the call.

Once again he regretted not having access to his Agency's confidential cyber network. Without it, only their near-field private comms with their nominally secure encrypt-decrypt coding protocols were safe—and then only over very short distances. For this he'd have to piggyback on the public network and expose them to possible snooping. At least here in the hotel he could link to that public network through the hotel's internal service systems, like he had with the elevator. Still a risk, though.

Well, they'd just have to keep it short. He made the connection.

Jeanne responded immediately. "Are you in?"

"No. There's two guards covering the door. It's those toad characters."

A slight pause. "Leonore's personal guard. Do not approach!"

"Maybe if I distract them...."

"No! Don't even think of trying it. We'll find another way."

"How? The only other entrance is the outside balcony. And we're nine-hundred-twenty floors up."

"Yeah, a bit of climb."

"And a heck of a drop!"

"Well this messes up our plans. Those mercenaries are known for standing their ground and not budging. Darn that Leonore! We may have to abort the mission. Unless...."

"What are you thinking? Nothing crazy I hope."

"I'll let you know. Stay where you are. Get out of sight, but don't move."

"Jeanne?" But she'd logged off.

Feeling uneasy, Gates checked the hallway and the two guards again, then settled down to wait.

* * * *

Jeanne sat alone in the cabin of the ground cab she and Gates had taken from the consulate, typing in commands on a touch-screen terminal provided for passengers, avoiding the more usual cyber-neural comm links or even the plug-in adapters for those not fortunate enough to be outfitted with modern conveniences. The automated cab patiently racked up charges on the government's tab—Roingroing had ordered it on the consulate's general expense account, keeping all their identities off the record so the trip wouldn't flag special notice from any nosy types inordinately interested in them leaving the protection of "foreign soil."

Using an anonymous shadow account and some unofficial tricks of the trade she'd picked up here and there—unofficial enough that she felt sure even her Agency wouldn't be wise to them—she got on a social platform called Yecks (formerly Blabber), selected private chat, audio only, disabled all tracking, then keyed in the handle Trix-One-Oh-Oh-Two-Nine. In the "from" field she wrote "Jeanne and sidekick."

It took a minute, but then that unmistakable light but confident voice came on. "Hello?"

"Trix! Remember me? Jeanne."

"O' course I remember you. I gave you my handle didn't I? What's with the audio only?"

"Not important right now. Look, did you mean it when you offered to help?"

"I did. Unlike some people I know—and by people I mean humans—I don't make empty promises."

"Then I need you now. You and your flyer."

"That's it? No how-do-you-do, Trix? How's things going, Trix?"

"Uh, small talk later. Right now I need to hire you."

"In that case, you're in luck. I just happen to be between fares. Where do you want me?"

"Do you know...sorry, of course you know. I'll be at parking ramp Cee a block behind the Stellar-Hyatt Hotel. Top deck. How soon can you get there?"

"Under ten minutes."

"Great. See you then."

"Should I bring anything? Somehow I get the feeling you might need more than just my virtuoso transportation acumen." In the background Jeanne could hear the sound of those wings thrumming up to speed.

"Thanks, but no. I'm okay for the moment."

"On my way then."

Jeanne signed off and directed the cab to take her to the top of the parking structure she'd indicated. Then she waited.

It didn't take long. The little insect-like machine separated out of city traffic, banked in low and with a soft flutter of wings descended into an empty parking slot. Jeanne got out of her cab and jogged over.

Trix rolled the canopy open. "Nice to see you again. A little curious about why."

Jeanne climbed in. "Take us up."

"Right to business. Okay, then." As they lifted off Trix said. "So where to?"

"I need you to fly me up there." Jeanne pointed up the side of the Stellar-Hyatt.

"Where?"

"My room. On the nine-hundred-twentieth floor."

"Nine-hundred-twenty...oof! Are you serious? That's getting close to my flyer's maximum ceiling! And where am I supposed to land?"

"You're not. I just need you to hover alongside the balcony."

"Oh right. And then what? You going to jump?"

"Yes."

"Holy...you're nuts! Do you know the kind of wind sheer I have to deal with up there?"

"I'm sure 'the best pilot on the planet' can handle it."

Trix looked up at the looming height of the sky-high building. "Uh, I may have oversold my skills just a little. You realize that's like a mile-and-a-half up!"

"A little more, actually."

Trix held the flyer close to the hotel's base, just above the first-story "jumper" apron that protected the ground level from falling objects. "Don't you need oxygen to live up there?"

"It's getting close to that point. But they do pump a little extra into the ventilation on those upper floors. Can we get going, please?"

"You couldn't have gotten a room a little lower, say only a *mile* high?"

"The reservation was made by my Agenc...I mean my embassy, paid up a month in advance. That's why it's still registered in my name."

Trix craned her neck up at the face of the hotel again. "So what's wrong with using the room's regular door?"

"I'd rather not get into that."

"Uh-huh. I suppose that's all you're gonna say on the subject."

"Can we table the matter for later? Just get me in close, open the canopy, and I'll do the rest." Jeanne hoped she sounded more self-confident than she felt.

Trix shook her head. "No. I can't let you do it. This is just too crazy. We're friends now, right? I can't let friends do dumb things."

"I appreciate that, Trix. But I have to. It's important, really important. Not just to me but to all of us. The survival of your whole world depends on it. Of all worlds, actually. There's people and politics at play that...well, you'll just have to believe me on this."

Trix studied her face. "My whole world, huh? People and politics, huh?"

"I'm afraid so."

"I still think you're nuts. But...there's something about you, something I saw in you earlier, that makes me want to trust you for some reason. Probably against my better judgment. Maybe I'm a little crazy, too." She sighed. "You're not going to change your mind?"

"Can't."

"All right. If that's how it's gotta be. Hold on, we're going vertical." The engines whined as she put the little craft into a steep climb.

As they approached their dubious destination the high altitude really did strain the flyer's capabilities. The wings hummed and labored, and strong winds funneling past the hotel's surface buffeted them relentlessly.

"It's the sixteenth balcony from the northeast corner," Jeanne advised.

Trix nosed them up to the designated balcony railing, the flyer bucking and bobbing from wind gusts, wings working fiercely to keep them aloft. She did her best to hold them close without smashing into the side of the building and opened the canopy.

"Watch that first step!" she shouted over the noise of the wind and wings. "But if you fall, I was never here!"

"If I fall you don't get a five-star rating!"

"Ha! You'd better not fall. I still expect to get paid!"

Jeanne assessed her chances. Not so good. Was the building swaying? Could be. Didn't they build flexibility into really tall structures like this? She gulped at the disorienting sensation.

Maybe this wasn't such a brilliant idea after all. Okay, slight change in plans. Only one sure way to make this jump, even if it meant disclosing her identity as Astra Woman. She released her safety harness and hung on precariously while activating her sens-suit and rejuvenation. As her transformation began she yelled back, "Uh, if you notice anything strange happening right now, just ignore it."

Trix's eyes grew big. "Ha! I figured there was more to you than you let on!"

A wind blast just then lifted them up and back. Jeanne barely caught herself in the canopy opening, instinctively looked down at the unprotected drop. Holy crap, that was a long, *loooong* way! She swallowed and tried to still her racing heart.

She let the flyer steady out while trying not to look down again (though she couldn't help herself—nope, not a good idea).

Trix fought with her controls, called out, "Whatever you're gonna do, you'd better do it fast. I can't hold us here forever!"

Jeanne reached inward for that stable calm center her meditations had showed her, reminded herself what was at stake—and that her suit and rejuvenation gave her extra strength and agility. She timed the flyer as it bucked forward once more, and jumped.

She overshot and hit the balcony's unbreakable glass door full front-on with a hard thump. Ouch. The suit protected everything but her nose. She rubbed it while hoping the guards out in the hallway hadn't heard. Luckily the hotel's suites had good sound proofing.

She collected her wits, turned and waved at Trix, who nodded in sympathetic relief and rolled her craft away and down to drop back into the main traffic of the city far below, leaving Jeanne alone on the little windy balcony.

Now to get in. Had she locked the balcony door before they left? Or would it just slide open....

Nope. Definitely locked.

Fortunately her sens-suit's extra strength let her force the lock without much difficulty, balcony doors not being the most secure things in the world.

All right. Step one, get inside the room—check. Nose slightly bruised but otherwise in one piece.

Goo suit still on the floor where she'd left it—check. The presence of the guards had probably kept room service out.

Briefly she thought to stuff some of her clothes and things into a travel bag and bring that along, but then clucked at herself. No unnecessary diversions or baggage, Jeanne! Stay on mission.

She tugged a little carry-pack around from the small of her back and drew a folded-up brown cloth from it, shook that out. This next part would require stealth, and the shadow cloak gave her just what she needed.

She gathered up the goo suit, crammed it into the empty carry-pack and repositioned it behind her. Then she called Gates on their private comms. They should be close enough now that they had direct connection. "Gates, are you there?"

She could almost see him perk up. "Yes! Where are you?"

"In our room. Don't ask me how. Those guards still there?"

"You know it."

"Get ready to distract them. I'm coming out."

"Oh boy! You want casual commotion or full blown riot?"

"Uh, something in between. Be creative. And watch yourself. Those fellows aren't known for being gentle."

"Right. Ready?"

"Go for it."

Jeanne threw the shadow cloak over her head, activated it, then stepped to the door's security panel. The monitor showed the backs of the two guards up close, their muscular toad necks right under the camera. She leaned in to the door. Through her sens-suit's extended perceptions, linked directly into the cyber-neural circuitry in her head, she could feel through the walls, sense each of the guards' double hearts beating, almost hear them breathing.

On the security monitor one of the guards moved suddenly off camera. She heard a muffled shout, a loud bark, then heavy footsteps running away.

She took that as her cue, cracked the door. The second guard still stood at his post, looking off down the hall at the other guard who limped angrily after Gates, a fresh bite wound in its meaty leg.

Jeanne suppressed a scolding chuckle and slipped out. Moving silently, she slid along the wall toward a connecting hallway several doors away.

Meanwhile the guard who'd remained at his station turned back, noticed the room door ajar and came to sudden alertness. Jeanne stood still.

The guard gave a suspicious look up and down the hallway. Not seeing anything, he threw the door fully open and stomped inside.

Jeanne took advantage and made a break for the adjoining hallway. She called Gates. "Gates, you okay?"

"Why wouldn't I be? This guy can't keep up even if he had two good legs. How about you?"

"For the moment. Do you have a safe way off this floor?"

"One of the service elevators like I came up on. You'll have to follow the hallways around. They're laid out in a square, a repeating pattern of eight squares to a floor. Just stick to the first one you're in. I'll meet you as you come around."

"What about that guard after you?"

"I'm leading him on a wild goose chase. As soon as you're clear I'll take off in a sprint, leave him in the dust—or the carpet fibers. That's assuming he doesn't give up before then. It must be dawning on him that he's abandoned his duty post, a serious no-no for his type, I'm thinking."

"Way to come through in a pinch, Gates! Did I ever tell you we make a good team?"

"I know, right?"

"Okay, I'm approaching the second turn in the hallway square now."

"Starting my sprint. Oops, a couple of guests are leaving their room...uh-oh, I might have accidentally tripped one up."

"Gates!"

"Too late now. Coming around the next turn."

"I see you."

"I don't see you. Oh wait, you're using the shadow cloak, aren't you? I can just make it out. Keep coming, watch for an intersecting service corridor ahead of you."

"Got it." Jeanne picked up the pace, met Gates at the corridor entrance. They hurried along it to the elevator at the end. Gates worked his cyber-hacking magic, and soon they were on their way down, nonstop to the main lobby.

* * * *

Getting to the swimming pool on the other side of the hotel, however, was another matter. Fortunately they could use maintenance and service corridors most of the way, only crossing main hallways intermittently.

They had to be even more careful now, though. While they'd run into only a few guests and service bots upstairs, down here in the common areas such encounters were unavoidable. Not to mention all the security cameras sprouting from every wall and ceiling.

As before, they kept together under the shadow cloak to avoid detection, moving slowly and relying on every species' typical inattentiveness to anything but themselves when going about their personal business. Once a small human child spotted them, or the wavy outline of their cloak anyway, but her impatient parents pulled her along the hall without giving her young inquisitiveness any attention.

Gates had to hack three more security door locks on the way. But eventually they made it to one of the guest changing rooms next to the pool, where their service corridor connected to a custodial storeroom full of fresh towels and cleaning supplies, and smells of disinfectant and pool chemicals mixed with the unmistakably strong stench of the goo-beings' slime wafting from farther in.

They did a brief check of the showers and locker area, but the changing room appeared empty. Evidently Leonore had not only put a stop to the ceremonial activities but also shooed everyone nonessential out—save for a dozen of her personal mercenary guards. Jeanne noted them as she peeked out into the main pool room, all gathered at one end of the pool in somewhat of a competitive standoff with the loyal security team Roingroing had put in place, still posted vigilantly around the red velvet ropes at the pool edge, a mix of species including several humans. Beyond them a small remnant of dedicated press corps congregated uncertainly in one corner.

Leonore herself was nowhere in sight. But from the disposition of the guards and press it seemed likely she'd already entered the pool.

Jeanne sluffed off the shadow cloak, pulled the goo suit out of her carry-pack, replaced it with the rolled-up cloak, then hid the pack on a high shelf behind a stack of towels. This time she put the goo suit on over her sens-suit and stayed in her rejuvenated Astra Woman state. That should give her more protection, and maybe even more sensing ability.

As she finished preparations she said, "I need another distraction. Can you get all the guards' attention directed toward the far end of the pool? Then I should be able to slip into this end without being spotted."

"That's a big gamble. What if you're seen?"

"No one else out there has a goo suit. Once I'm in the pool I'm good. My biggest worry is that *you* stay safe. Those toadies are carrying zapper pistols."

"So I play it like I'm just a stray animal who happened to wander in."

"You are anything but *just* an animal, my loyal and brave friend! As you consistently prove over and over."

"But *they* don't know that. All sentient species we interact with learn that dogs are humankind's best friends, but we're 'just' animals to them. As long as they think I'm not a threat—or a spy—they'll simply treat me as a nuisance."

"I suppose that *is* kind of the whole point of keeping your genetically augmented nature a secret. And you play the part of the 'dumb animal' so well."

"Hey!"

"Kidding. All right, I trust your judgment. We'll give it a go."

"You're lucky I'm so forgiving or I'd take that crack personally. Instead I'm going to be the devoted partner, mosey out there like I own the place and get them all to focus on me—which shouldn't be hard since I'm so cute."

"Oh-ho! Nice one. But true. Let's do this." She pulled her suit's flexible hood over her head and pressed the neck seal tight.

Gates stuck his nose out of the changing room, then headed out: to all intents and purposes a curious but misplaced animal, someone's lost emotional-support pet.

The security detail around the pool paid little attention to him, but the toad mercenaries took more notice of Gates's intrusion into their perimeter of protection. They watched him saunter casually toward them, sniffing random objects along the way. Several pointed their zapper pistols at him while he wandered untroubled around behind them. One tried to wave him off, and Gates used that as an excuse to start barking, thereby converging the guards' attention even more strongly on him.

Jeanne got set to dash out (conjuring up the childhood phrase "No running in the pool!" in her head, though she quickly quashed it with "Not now, childhood brain!").

Gates had the toadies engaged as fully as he could. He shouted "Now!" on their comms, and she made a break for the pool.

Now if Roingroing had done his part, which of course he had, he would have messaged his guards to expect someone in such a suit with the Council's gold circle emblem emblazoned on its collar and let that person through.

Those loyal guards came to alertness, but then nodded and let her pass.

She hurriedly stooped to sit on the edge, slipped her legs into that viscous goop—already feeling familiar electric tingles—took one more glance to see if Gates was okay, then let go her forebodings, held her breath (unnecessarily) and slid in all the way.

Chapter 4

Prickly energy patterns and filtered greenish light engulfed her once again, and those pellucid gelatinous gummy-worm bodies swirled around her, evidently surprised at her sudden unannounced entrance into their midst.

But they quickly quieted down as they recognized her, greeting her with a sensation of welcome, which she returned in kind. The experience felt friendly and cordial this time, almost familial in a strangely comforting way. While her translation software was still defective, she no longer felt she needed it with them.

Across the pool, however, some distance away and indistinct through the thickish liquid, another dark human shape hung suspended. It looked like Leonore had taken on her own rejuvenated state under her goo suit. Jeanne tried one of the Council's standard comm channels, hoping that at this range it would get through just like her private channel with Gates. "Leonore!"

The response came promptly—though accompanied by odd static, probably interference from the Gu'gundreans' electrical-alkaline medium. "Well, Jeanne, I wondered if you'd show up. Oh yes, we intercepted your earlier comm with your SPOT companion—using the public net was a bit careless of you, but then I suppose that's really my fault, isn't it, for shutting you out of everything else? Your break-in upstairs drew notice pretty quickly, too, from hotel security and law enforcement. You took quite a chance. I'll give you '*A*' for effort, but I wasn't entirely sure you'd make it from there."

"Stop what you're doing. I'm not going to let you harm the Gu'gundreans!"

"Harm them? Is that what you think? That's the furthest thing from my intentions. I want to learn from them, learn their unique technology. That's the key!"

Jeanne felt a little thrown. "The key?"

"Let me turn off my translator so we keep this private. Yes, the key—to everything! To the Final Plan."

"You mean your plan to destroy galaxies if everyone doesn't bow to your will?"

"Oh, naïve Jeanne. You do not understand the grand picture."

"I guess not. And what technology? The Gu'gundreans have no hands or any way to manipulate materials to build technology."

"Tsk, I'm surprised at you. Such a limited, human-centric way of looking at things. Let me educate you. Yes, we think of technology as mechanical or electronic devices, because that's what we make, it's what we know. The same goes for other intelligent species with gripping appendages. But the Gu'gundreans have such a distinctive biology and environment that they've had to develop something entirely different, something all their own, a way to directly manipulate *chemicals* on a biological and molecular level, without mechanical means, to create molecular technology! They can fabricate compounds, both organic and inorganic, that we can't even dream of."

"Interesting. I hadn't thought of them that way. But what's that got to do with this key you say they have?"

"Everything! Look, how old would you say their adults are?"

"I don't know, I never asked."

"I'll tell you. *Very* old."

"Sure, I know they trace their lineages way back—"

"No, it's more than that. Oral histories and legends make nice stories, but that's not enough to go on. We've taken cell samples. Are you familiar with certain plants on earth that seem to have no programmed senescence? Their cells can in theory go on living forever, or clones of them anyway, as they regenerate. Unless something destroys the entire organism, they are essentially immortal."

"I've heard of that. A lot of research went into trying to figure out how to use that to extend human life. I believe it's even the basis of our own Agency's rejuvenation technique."

"It is—well, a sort of mechanical nano-bot version of it, anyway."

"But as I recall, that's as far as anyone could take it. And it has long-term adverse consequences, too, as we both know. It could never be used permanently, or be adapted for general use."

"Exactly. That's mainly because those plants evolved over many millions of years, with unique biological characteristics specific only to them. They don't transfer well to other species, especially from plant to animal."

"So how are the Gu'gundreans any different? Aside from the fact that they're not plants. Uh, they aren't, are they?"

"No. The difference is that they've developed their techniques *deliberately*—even scientifically although their science is unrecognizable to us—through chemical manipulation, molecular technology. Which means they know exactly what's involved, how to create it and how to alter it or adapt it for other uses. Do you see what that means? They hold the key to their own longevity—to creating immortality! Not just for them but for others."

"Hmm. And you have this immortality technology now?"

"Not yet. That's why we have to work with them, get them on our side."

"And then what? Everyone gets to be immortal?"

"Well, no. First, it wouldn't be *actual* immortality. That's an impossibility even in theory since everything runs down—the law of entropy—even the universe itself eventually. It's just a very long extended life. And second, there are practical barriers, like an ever-expanding population and problems housing and feeding everyone and so on. So it would have to be restricted to a select few highly qualified leaders and elites."

"Like you."

"Is that sarcasm? Yes, me. Who better to be in charge, to direct everything? Who else has the experience, the knowledge, the will?"

Jeanne shook her head. "What happened to you, Leonore? I used to look up to you. You used to be a beacon of all the good the Council stands for. Have you forgotten the Council's mission? This Golden Circle emblem on or our uniforms means something! Its not just an empty symbol!"

"Ah, but a circle *is* empty. There's literally nothing inside it."

Huh.

Leonore went on, "But you've got me all wrong. I still believe in those values, in the Council's goal and mission. Don't you see? I've worked my whole life toward that goal! Yet you must realize that the Council is ineffective—like that circle, an empty symbol. It can do very little the way it is."

"So change it from within."

"Oh, I've tried, believe me. Many times and in many ways. Yet in all my long years of service the one thing I've learned is that there's only one way to bring about true peace throughout the universe. And that's through total control and authority. And the only way to do that is through total power."

"Total power. Like destroying galaxies?"

"An unfortunate but necessary sacrifice—and one that pains me deeply, I assure you. But it's only for the greater good. Once peace is established in the universe through knowledge that any violation can result in the annihilation of an entire galaxy, there will be no more wars or killing."

"And you don't see the irony in that?"

"I see it as a hard reality: desperate problems, drastic solutions."

Wow. A fanatical ideologue, a "true believer." How do you reason with someone like that?

Jeanne felt out her energy connection with the Gu'gundreans, urgently asked them to look into Leonore' mind, try to find out the details of her plan if they could, like where she had this galaxy-destroying device hidden.

Meantime she needed to stretch out the conversation. "I still don't get it. Are you really that power hungry?"

"Power hungry? Or Altruistic."

"Altruistic! That's what you call this Plan of yours?"

"Semantics. Call it benevolent dictatorship. Or peace through fear if you must."

"Peace through fear? Is that seriously what you want your legacy to be? I mean, peace through strength, sure, that's understandable. But *fear?*"

"Fear is the greatest motivator."

"Oh? How about love? Compassion? Empathy? Or just the desire to live a good life and let others live theirs? Live and let live!"

"Ah, Jeanne, so innocent. All those grand platitudes are meaningless. The universe is ruthless. It cares nothing for love and compassion—or even whether we live or not. The same is true of most people when it comes down to their most basic drives. Whether you admit it or not, fear is the greatest motivator."

"Debatable. But even if the universe is ruthless, that doesn't mean *we* have to be. You used to believe in human goodness, and living in harmony with other beings. And that we could spread goodwill and create that peaceful universe you want through peaceful means, by showing compassion and open friendship. And leading by example."

"I was young. I've learned. The lessons have been hard, harsh and unyielding, but in the end undeniable."

Jeanne tried to wrap her head around this warped logic, couldn't. "And this galaxy-eating weapon, you just happened to develop that right now, too? Coincidentally at the same time we discovered the Gu'gundreans?"

"Oh no. We've had that for well over a decade. It's actually an extension of sub-quantum dimensional collapse technology, just taken to an extreme. But we didn't dare use it because of one major roadblock: What would happen if I'd used it before? I'd establish peace in the universe, but for how long? Until I die? Then who takes over? What guarantee do I have that they'll be as far-sighted and selfless as I am?"

"Selfless! There you go again. And who's this 'we' you keep mentioning?"

"A few trusted acolytes—I mean lieutenants—who've come to see things the way I do. But as I was saying, the Plan remained only a distant dream, an 'if only' fantasy— until we encountered the Gu'gundreans and saw that they hold the key to making it work! A way for one morally righteous person to stay in charge indefinitely and ensure the long-term viability of the Plan."

"You do know there've been other 'benevolent dictators'

in history. It never worked out—for the people o*r* the dictator."

"Only this time I'll have what they didn't—absolute power!"

"Oh yes. And we know that absolute power never corrupts, right?"

"Bah. You're thinking is small. You have no vision, no image of the glorious future I'm offering."

"Offering or inflicting? Free people have rejected your kind of offer many times before. Just like I am now."

"Too bad. I'd hoped to bring you around to some measure of understanding, to see the true path to peace in the universe, maybe even to join us. But you've shown yourself pitifully incapable of that. Disappointingly so. And now this conversation has become pointless and tedious. So leave. I still have things to discuss with the Gu'gundreans."

"I'm not leaving. I won't let you do this."

"Don't bother trying anything against me. I came prepared. My sens-suit is an upgraded version of yours. More strength, more quickness, and much greater electrical resistance should these initial talks with the Gu'gundreans prove less than hospitable."

"Speaking of that...." Jeanne switched her attention to her energy connection with the Gu'gundreans, asked if they've found anything out.

They had. And it made them very agitated.

In that momentary interlude Leonore realized belatedly that she'd been so engrossed in conversation she'd left herself open in other ways. Now she sensed something probing her mind: the Gu'gundreans—somehow they'd violated her innermost privacy! And done so in complicity with this upstart Jeanne! How had she done that? Her translator had been deliberately incapacitated.

But no denying it: she'd already gotten to them, already

swayed them to her side. While Leonore had been patiently, even maternally trying to mentor her underling, the ungrateful brat had been secretly working behind her back to turn the Gu'gundreans against her and thwart her efforts to win their trust and cooperation. For now anyway.

Outraged, Leonore flew up out of the pool.

* * * *

Jeanne thanked the Gu'gundreans for their help, exchanging good energy flows. Then she climbed out of her end of the pool and stood dripping soupy glop on the tiles.

At the opposite end Leonore had removed the hood from her goo suit, shaken out her wavy black hair, and while still in her rejuvenated youngish state glared wrathfully at her adversary. But with the press still present, and Roingroing's guards moving in now to shield Jeanne, Leonore and her toadies couldn't risk a public clash.

Infuriated, she stalked off.

Gates padded around to Jeanne's side.

Jeanne pulled her own hood off, said, "There's my good boy! Are you all right?"

"Didn't even work up a sweat—whatever that means since dogs don't sweat. Those clowns are too big and clumsy to catch me! Did you learn anything?"

"Besides the fact that I won't be getting a bonus from the Council this year?" Jeanne's features darkened. "Oh I learned a few things, Gates. More than you imagine. And it's bad. *Very* bad!"

"Oh?"

"Let me hit the showers and rinse the stink off this suit. I need to sit down, too. I'm suddenly pretty tired." She turned to head back into the changing room, staggered a little.

Gates looked at her with concern. "Uh-oh. You've stayed in rejuvenation mode too long."

"Yeah, guess I'm starting to feel the effects."

"You'd better deactivate your Astra Woman persona immediately. Then we need to get you back to Roingroing's consulate so you can rest up awhile."

"Rest sounds nice." She reversed her rejuvenation. "And food, I need fuel. I'm thinking chicken enchiladas."

"Off the subject! And I'm pretty sure the Spraang don't have anything like that."

"Hey, this is my food fantasy, don't interrupt. Now where was I? Oh yes, chicken enchiladas with sour cream and...."

"Can we stick to what you learned from Leonore?"

"Spoil sport." Jeanne entered the showers and turned on a hot, steamy, full-force spray. "Okay, so it turns out she didn't have a clue that the Gu'gundreans could connect directly with our minds by matching energy flows. Or that they can do the same with our standard electronic communications and listen in there, too—something even I didn't know. I imagine that was the static I got on our comms when she and I were talking. From the impression they gave me they actually heard everything, though with their alien way of communicating and thinking it may take them awhile to process and interpret it all. For that matter, *I* may need awhile to process and interpret it all."

"What about the galactic-goodbye device?"

"Oh yes. We're looking for that, aren't we? How do you feel about a trip off world? Um, that's not a very clear answer, is it? My thinking's getting a little fuzzy. Guess I really do need some rest. Can we wait until we get back to the consulate and I've had a chance to recuperate a little? Then I can go over it all with both you and Roingroing when my brain's working right."

"Is your brain ever working right?"

"Ha ha. Is this going to become a thing with us now? I

insult you, you insult me?"

"Hey, you started it. And I'm just a 'dumb animal,' remember?"

"But cute."

Gates spun around in a circle. "That I am!"

* * * *

After her shower Jeanne reclaimed her carry pack with the shadow cloak inside, rolled up the goo suit, and with what seemed the last of her energy asked four of Roingroing's guards to escort them out to the loading loop where a Spraang diplomatic vehicle waited.

They encountered no interference. Jeanne suspected Leonore must be reassessing things after their meeting just as much as she was, so they might have a little reprieve before Ms. Big and Bad regrouped and acted again.

Back at the consulate Jeanne dragged herself to their visitor's quarters and flopped down on the spongy cushion the Spraang provided. Gates pulled a coverlet over her and defended the entrance to make sure no one disturbed her.

Several hours later Jeanne woke feeling fresh but famished. She called up the consulate kitchen to order room service. No, they didn't have chicken enchiladas, whatever those were. Jeanne selected a cheese omelet with synth-sausage, cauliflower, and blueberry yogurt. She needed protein to regenerate. Also a balanced meat-and-gravy total-nutrition dog meal for Gates. At least those were all on the consulate's regular "human" guest menu.

Feeling renewed, they convened again with Roingroing in the meditation dome in the back-lot garden.

"I've ressspected your ressstorative sssleep ssscycle," he began immediately, "but I'm anxiousss to dissscover the ressultsss of your misssion."

Jeanne sank onto the cushion-floor, marveling at the

contrast between this mellow red-lit environment and the Gu'gundreans' watery green goop, each very different but each strangely tranquil in its own way, now that she'd gotten used to both.

She drew a breath. "Well, it seems Leonore has upped the ante. Uh, that means she's raised the stakes, Roingroing, elevated the danger. Instead of planting the galaxy-destroying device in some small, sparsely-populated galaxy for another anonymous demonstration like we expected, she's actually going to plant it right here in *our* galaxy."

Roingroing let out a squeal. "Why would ssshe do thisss?"

"I'm not sure. Possibly she thinks she's been exposed now, and that's changed her whole calculus, forced her to more desperate measures. The Gu'gundreans only told me that the device is being secretly readied for deployment at a star a few light-years from here. Apparently it's rather large and has to be assembled and finalized on site, then dropped into a star of at least one-hundred solar masses in order to work—something to do with needing a sufficient mass to jump start the larger collapse process. They also said it's triggered by a remote mechanism Leonore keeps in a secret location, since she doesn't trust anyone else to carry out her threat."

"That fitsss with sssomething I learned today while you ssslept, from covert leaksss in high esschelonsss. All very husssh-husssh, but it ssseemsss Leonore hasss ssstarted contacting leadersss of sssome governmentsss with her demandsss, sssending them the videosss of her tessstsss. Ssshe's no longer conssscealing herssself."

"Oh? What's been their response?"

"At thisss ssstage, I think disssbelief mossstly."

"Sure, typical bureaucratic incompetence and inaction. They're going to totally blow it, even when they do get around to doing anything. And with someone as fanatical as Leonore, that's almost guaranteed to be fatal—for all of us in this case." She creased her brow. "So we can't rely on them, they don't even know the real story of what Leonore is all about. No, if she's going to be stopped, it's up to us to do it."

"There'sss that 'usss' again! Ssshouldn't we go to our ressspective governmentsss and tell them what we've dissscovered?"

"Do you really think they'd believe us? Neither of us is particularly prominent or important. And as far as the authorities know, I've been tagged a fugitive since shortly after I got here. I just broke into the Stellar-Hyatt hotel for unauthorized trespassing and invasion of an official alien delegation's protected area. You've had questionable dealings with me as well as not-so-legal contact with clandestine sources who shared classified materials you shouldn't have access to. If we do manage to get the governments to take us seriously, they're going to vet us to the nth degree, interrogate us for weeks, subject us to psych analyses and who knows what all. By then it will be too late."

"That sssoundsss hopelesss! And exssstremely unpleasssant."

"If we go that route, yes. Which is why we won't. No, we only have one real option." She nodded decisively. "Roingroing, we're going to need another ride. Something a little bigger this time and with a star drive in it."

* * * *

Gates trotted along beside Jeanne. "So you condensed all that down earlier to just 'How do you feel about a trip off world?'"

"Seems so. My mind works in mysterious ways when I'm tired."

Roingroing bounced on ahead as they approached a small

courier spacecraft the Spraang kept in another on-site dome that served as garage for three or four such vehicles. The craft—vibrant pink, naturally—wasn't *much* bigger than a taxi, Jeanne thought. When she'd said a "little bigger" she should have realized Roingroing would take that literally. It looked something like a partially flattened sphere or maybe chicken egg (she still had chicken enchiladas on her mind).

They climbed through a side opening into a cramped cabin obviously designed for Spraang: barely high enough for a bent-over human if the person stayed on hands and knees, no seats but four half-spherical cushions contoured to fit Spraang shapes. Gates could curl up in one nicely but Jeanne had to scrunch backward into hers with knees nearly up to her chin. Her carry pack with the shadow cloak in it pressed into the small of her back; maybe she should have left that behind—but no, that cloak had already come in handy, and likely would again.

She wriggled uncomfortably. "Where are the safety harnesses?"

"Sssafety harnesssesss? We Ssspraang have no need of sssuch thingsss. We're our own air bagsss." Roingroing took a forward pilot position, extended five or six pseudopods and began tapping at a curving control panel molded seamlessly into the walls of the craft. Jeanne couldn't tell which controls did what, since everything looked pretty much the same: monotonous pink with little patterns of bumps that reminded her more of Braille than anything mechanical.

The side door slid closed, they felt a change in air pressure, and the little ship shuddered as it raised off the garage floor. To the front the curved hull became transparent, and through it they could see the garage dome opening like the petals of a flower, revealing glittering capitol buildings all around reaching into the sky and reflecting orange rays from the setting sun. Roingroing guided them up and out, negotiating city traffic to a dedicated downtown launch corridor, where he merged with a line of other small craft hitching a free lift on the magnetic "updraft" provided by the local space control and customs service. (Actually, not so free, seeing as how taxes and vehicle registration fees paid for it.)

He engaged his craft's own magnetic monopole generator, matching polarity with the ground beam for repulsion and carrying them swiftly aloft. Below, the planet's carefully curated lands spread out on all sides, rapidly diminishing to become a curving planetary hemisphere clothed in a thin veneer of atmosphere.

Once high above it all and clear of other traffic, the onboard computer verified destination and navigation and Roingroing kicked in the sub-quantum FTL drive—compressing ordinary dimensions and uncurling quantum ones, manipulating their quantumly-superposed and entangled states in an extremely precise way, so that after only a minor shift among those compressed dimensions they could reverse the process and rebound into normal space at a meticulously calculated point: this one a moderately short hop of some forty-three light years.

Ahead a class F bluish star shone brightly several AU's distant. Roingroing checked his coordinates, corrected for the star's proper motion within the galaxy, located the planet they wanted called Serebus IV, corrected to match its orbital motion, then overlaid an image of commercial approach-departure corridors to make sure he steered clear of them. Finally he made his second jump to within half a planetary radius.

Fortunately they could rely on a unique property of sub-quantum FTL travel: its natural abhorrence of mass, the need to operate away from planetary masses and even other ships. If you came out of dimensional compression too near another ship or other object, the two masses would simply repel each other, so there could never be any collisions— something like the Pauli exclusion principle for particles applied to large collections of particles (like ships), or the idea that two masses can't occupy the same space at the same time. The worst that could happen was two ships would jostle each other a bit in passing (sometimes *quite* a bit). But since most people, especially commercial carriers and paying customers on passenger ships, didn't like that, pilots still had to conform to basic space courtesy and rules of the road.

Of course, once you'd come fully out of dimensional compression and shut down the drive, all bets about collisions were off.

Roingroing coasted nearer by sight and by instrument while arranging landing clearance with ground control, finally entering the atmosphere above the main space port and gliding into the magnetic lift corridor's "down" lane to blend with other traffic coming and going.

Below, Serebus IV wasn't nearly so populous as the teeming cultural and political center of Lystrom Two they'd just left. Basically a mining and manufacturing hub, this city had built up around the space port and reflected that less glamorous and more workaday world, a hard practicality and no-nonsense pragmatism manifested in the somewhat squat and uninspired architecture made largely of ultra-hardened concrete and tinted glass refined from local earth and rock.

Yet it had it's own picturesque character, Jeanne thought as they settled onto a paved landing lot among scores of other small craft of countless shapes and designs, like a collection of mis-matched Christmas ornaments laid out on the ground. Larger ships occupied berths not far away beyond a row of warehouses, their hulls looming above the rooftops.

Jeanne noticed the air's smell first thing as they got out of the courier craft: more minerally, less citified than her usual haunts, and a bit dusty. But then, this wasn't a forested world or an agricultural one, nor an ocean one nor an over-developed urban-sprawl planet-wide metropolis either.

A port robo-transport pulled up—an open-air cart, really, with bench seats for eight or ten passengers. They got in and started off for the port entry and customs office across the landing field. Jeanne activated her Astra Woman guise on the way, but wore a belted aquamarine robe over her sens-suit so that her ambassador/secret-agent status wouldn't be recognized and reported to any unfriendlies who might still be on the lookout for her.

Fortunately Roingroing's diplomatic pass gave them expedited processing, just a simple body scan and statement of purpose and they were through. Things like IDs and e-passports didn't mean much in a galaxy where trillions and trillions of individuals came and went continually, where population dynamics shifted and people's life details changed far too often for any administrative system to keep up with. So such ineffective protocols had fallen out of use long ago. A few aborted attempts to substitute more invasive practices like mind probes or injecting everyone with genetic tags were greeted with public outcry and summarily voted down by free people, then outlawed permanently as part of the galactic covenants. Now travelers were just scanned for contraband and terrorist-type weapons. It made for an interesting if somewhat free-for-all social environment.

Once through customs and off port grounds Jeanne relaxed her rejuvenation to normal and they hailed a robo cab. The Gu'gundreans hadn't been able to give her actual names or anything else specific, just energy "pictures" or impressions, but she knew this was the right planet. And she knew it involved a government-sponsored entity engaged in mining, refining and exporting very rare raw materials for use in sub-quantum FTL technology. Made sense, if that same technology provided the basis for Leonore's galaxy-collapsing weapon.

She also knew that the government sponsor involved was really a front or proxy for the Council's behind-the-scenes doings.

What the Gu'gundreans *had* shown her, in the absence of a company name, was a logo image: a red starburst inside two crossed silver rings. Find the logo, find the company.

And what better place to start than a local watering hole where workers unwound and commiserated.

The robo cab had several common city attractions programmed into its nav system, including any number of liquid refreshment outlets. Jeanne decided (based on recent experience) to forego stim-inns and stick to more respectable taverns and pubs. They chose one likely prospect with high Yip ratings near the edge of town, where factories and mining operations began and spread into the barren countryside.

"Pigger's" seemed to do a lively business at all hours. On a street of mostly humble shops, it stood out with flashing lights and colorful signs depicting drinks and eats. They entered through a short mirrored and blacklit hallway— though Jeanne suspected it hid weapons scanners and numerous other security devices.

Inside, a multiplicity of species in assorted company uniforms mingled in what seemed a boisterous celebration and strange throbbing alien music.

Jeanne tapped the closest human participant on the shoulder. "What's the occasion?"

A brawny curly-headed woman in tan coveralls turned, exposing the logo on her lapel: a dragon riding a rocket, rodeo style. "Eh?"

Jeanne lifted her voice over the noise. "I said, something special going on?"

"Oh. Haven't you heard? Three separate teams just finished a major government contract today. Big bonuses all around. Whoo-oo!" She raised a large stein, sloshing liquid onto the floor and onto Jeanne's robe. Jeanne stepped back and brushed at the uninvited spillage. She liked this robe.

When she looked again the woman had melded back into the crowd. Meanwhile Roingroing shot a pseudopod up to the ceiling and pulled himself up to get a look over everyone's heads—or antennas or horns or humps or spiny backs as the case may be. He spotted a small group of other Spraang in a corner, and with a series of deftly-placed pseudopods swung over to them.

Jeanne shouldered her way to the bar, Gates keeping close to her side. A more subdued clientele there gave better chances for conversation. As she edged in, an order screen lit up on the bar in front of her with a list of automated offerings. She ignored it and nodded to the little bristly Shalukk female next to her, a species that, other than the black bristles covering their entire bodies, looked very much like an upright otter. They were also known for their sociability, and when tipsy, talkativeness.

Jeanne made a try at Trade Standard lingo. "Good trade day. You get bonus too?"

The Shalukk looked her over. "Human?"

Jeanne nodded.

"I speak human. You're new?"

By "human" she apparently meant English, conveniently for Jeanne. "Just got in. So all this for one Council...I mean one government contract?"

"Yeah. But only for *those* guys." She jerked an ottery thumb at the partiers on the main floor. "I wasn't part of their teams. No bonus for me or my pals here!" Her bristles rippled in a wave.

"Oh, too bad. Know anything about it, though?"

"Oh sure. Really big deal. Government big shots swooped in, paid top dollar for rush mine-refine job. Composite ore, hyper-dense superconducting magnetic monopole product. That's what *those* guys do. Special teams. Same stuff they turn out every day for sub-quantum use, only this time in massive quantity."

"That's interesting." Jeanne could guess what for, but wanted to find out the cover story Leonore had given. "Do you know why these government types would want that much so fast?"

"Who know? No one asks. A government pays, we produce. Or *some* of us do. Although come to think of it, everybody's been especially tight-lipped about this one." She saw something on the bar top. "Hey, you'd better order. You're screen's blinking red. You're going to get kicked out unless you buy something."

Jeanne checked the screen at her elbow, identical to the ones in front of every patron at the bar. Only hers flashed a red warning. Still unwilling to access electronic currency, and not wanting to expend her few remaining hard coins, she sped up the conversation. "Do you know where this special shipment went?"

"Do I look like I'm in management? Though I doubt anybody there knows either, except maybe the top boss of the whole operation."

Jeanne glimpsed a tall, hefty, anodized-steel robot bouncer parting the crowd, heading her way. She got up to go, asked hastily, "Do you know who this top boss might be?"

"Now there's a stumper. Could be someone in the government liaison office, or maybe in one of the three companies contracted to do the work."

The robot was almost to them. Jeanne got set to make a break for it. "Would one of those companies have a logo like a red starburst inside two crossed silver rings?"

"Yeah. How'd you know? That's Star-to-Star Technologies."

"Thanks!" Jeanne ducked out of the robot's grasp just in time and bolted for the exit, Gates right on her heels.

* * * *

Outside, they waited for Roingroing. He showed up shortly.

"I wasss keeping a visssual sssensssor on you. Why did you leave ssso fassst?"

"Turns out they have a two-drink minimum, and they're pretty strict about it. Did you learn anything?"

"The businesss we ssseek isss called Ssstar-to-Ssstar Technologiesss."

"That's the story I got, too. Anything more?"

"Their officesss are in the hillsss outsssside the csssity, at their exsssstraction and processssing inssstallation."

"Then that's where we're going."

They hailed another ground autocab on Roingroing's diplomatic credit, found the company's address among the cab's address listings, and set off.

On the way Roingroing asked, "Ssso what'sss our

ssstrategy?"

"Just walk in and ask nicely?"

"I sssussspect they will be lesss than forthcoming."

"Yeah. Well, I do have a few other tricks."

"I'm sssure of that, basssed on our recsssent hissstory. Sssomething to do with your sssecret ssside hussstle?"

"Sort of. Although I've got no backup now. I'm on my own."

"Hey," Gates piped up in her head. "What am I, dead weight?"

Jeanne patted Gates's side. "Except for my faithful protector here. Anyway, we have to take this one step at a time—or one bounce in your case. Let's just see how things go when we get there."

The rest of the trip they watched stark countryside whiz by: rocky hills and long sandy slopes, mostly browns and tans and earthy reds, with sporadic scraggly scrub and patchy dry grass straining feebly for survival. Occasional side roads branched off toward boxy factory complexes wedged in between peaks or set into valleys and plateaus carved out of the landscape.

Before long the cab slowed and turned onto one of those paved side roads, winding uphill past a sign bearing a glitzy logo of a red starburst inside two silver rings. Beneath that a promo slogan proclaimed: "Star-to-Star Technologies, wherever you're going, we get you there!" Then in smaller letters "sub-quantum materials mining, refining, fabricating—and lots of other nifty things."

At the top of the drive and near the peak of a high bluff they came to a stop at what must be the corporate offices, a series of glassed-in and dark-tinted cubes stacked in an offset pattern. Farther on, two or three sprawling low factory buildings crested the hill, with more trailing down the other side, hinting at just the tip of the company's holdings.

An inscription etched in artful silver and red on the office front stated, somewhat more sedately than before, "Star-to-Star Technologies, Serebus IV division."

They got out. "Gates," Jeanne said silently, "are you getting anything? We should be close enough now."

"Picking up lots of activity on private data bands. There's a local network between these offices and the factories. Their security firewalls are pretty tight, though. Not so easy to hack in here."

"Keep trying."

Roingroing spoke up. "Ssso how do we sssee thisss Top Bosss?"

"We don't. Like you said, they're not going to be forthcoming. And the top person certainly isn't going to drop everything to meet with unannounced and unknown visitors. We'll have to be more indirect, which means playing a part, an acting role, being untruthful about some things. And since that goes against your completely literal nature it's best if you keep quiet and leave all the talking—and the subterfuge—to me."

At that moment the main office door opened and a sleek reception robot rolled out, a plastic matt-gray cylinder about head high to Jeanne and balanced on a single unicycle wheel.

A flashing message on its front stated in Galactic Trade Standard: "Select language."

Jeanne scrolled through the displayed list until she found "human-English," pressed it.

The robot immediately responded with "Welcome to Star-to-Star Technologies. Do you have an appointment?"

Jeanne queried her canine conspirator. "Gates, we need

something to work with here, fast."

"I'm only into the lower-level admin systems. Best I can do is set us up with a basic factory tour."

"Better than nothing. Make it for Spraang representative and party."

"Okay, it's input, back-dated and scheduled for today. We're meeting with a PR exec named Sorz."

The robot repeated "Welcome to Star-to-Star Technologies. Do you have an appointment?"

"Uh, yes. We're here for our tour of your marvelous facilities. Representatives of the Spraang homeworld. They're thinking of expanding their dealings with your company. We're scheduled to meet with one of your VP's named Sorz."

The robot processed this information. "One moment. Mr. Sorz is running a little late. Please have a seat in our reception area."

They followed the machine through the main entrance into a spacious waiting lobby with a glossy black floor, ceiling-high darkened windows looking out on the hillside approach, and air pleasantly filtered and humidity-controlled. On the back wall several active displays hyped the company's products and production methods in colorful and professionally-produced marketing videos.

They took seats at universal blank-template furnishings that sensed and adjusted to each species' body shape. The robot rolled over and assumed position behind a standing desk or countertop.

"Gates," Jeanne inquired, "got anything more yet?"

"No. They really do have good security here. I'd almost swear they have some our Agency's proprietary classified stuff."

"That can't be. Unless...wait a minute. Leonore! She must

have had it installed secretly when she assigned them her 'government' contract."

"That'd be my guess. I can break in with my own Agency software, but only by using brute force. And that would give us away pretty quickly."

"So much for things being easy. I guess we'll have to make the best of this factory tour then, get what we can out of that."

Just then a small, three-foot-high rodent-like creature scuttled in on two legs from an inner hallway, looking harried, its charcoal business suit not quite fitting its furry form. It caught sight of the visitors and bustled over to them. "Terribly sorry! There seems to have been a glitch in our scheduling, and I wasn't informed...well, I suppose it's my fault for not keeping on top of these things...but you see there's only a few here who speak human English, and I see that was requested when you made the appointment...but of course that's entirely our problem, not yours...and now I'm rambling. Sorry again. Sorz. That's my name."

Jeanne stood. "Think nothing of it. We didn't mind waiting at all."

"You're very gracious. And may I say, we've always had a splendid relation with the Spraang, and look forward to expanding that association." He bowed courteously to Roingroing.

Jeanne drew his attention back to her. "Yes, well that's why we're here. At the request of the Spraang, as executive assistant I'll be acting as intermediary. Shall we get started?"

"Of course! This way." He waved a rodent paw out the front door, where a golf-cart-like vehicle had just pulled up.

On the ride over to the first factory building Sorz went into his standard spiel, touting the virtues of his company, it's award-winning quality control and innovation and productive speed and capacity, etc.

They exited the golf cart outside a walk-in entrance, where a buzzer sounded and a light above the door blinked green to allow admittance. "Most everything is automated, of course," Sorz continued as he ushered everyone into a receiving warehouse full of plastic shipping containers and robot forklifts moving about and stacking things in orderly high rows. "Live workers serve mainly as supervisors and overseers, and are provided with excellent, safe and sanitary environments." He indicated a line of glassed-in booths high up to one side.

Jeanne signaled Gates. "Anything noteworthy in here?"

"Not especially. This is just where they receive and store incoming materials, supplies, machinery."

She addressed their tour guide. "This is all well and good. But we're actually more interested in the output end of things."

"Yes, certainly. That starts in the next building. Follow me." He boarded a standing-only personnel carrier. They joined him and it immediately set off across the warehouse floor, evading other machinery and trundling over to the building's opposite end.

The carrier rolled through a connecting tunnel into another large space, where a series of massive gray machinery housings concealed inner workings, all humming loudly. Another set of glassed-in booths monitored events from on high.

"This is one of our lesser processing facilities," Sorz yelled over the noise as they cruised slowly past. "It's where secondary ore byproducts are refined, then funneled out for a variety of spin-off uses, everything from the super-focused magnetic monopole beam generators for spacecraft launch and landing, to elevator mag-lift systems, to robot power packs, to the little mini-motors in your home's automated furniture—even in your never-charge electric toothbrush."

"This is all impressive," Jeanne said. "But it's not really what we came to see."

"I understand. A little patience, please."

The personnel carrier glided through another connecting tunnel to a third factory building, this one populated with more glassed-in booths but on the ground floor and more like separate small cubes, each containing two or three workers busy at computers and other odd-looking equipment that Jeanne could only assume had something to do with materials analysis or systems control.

But what really grabbed their notice was what lay beneath this room's thick but transparent glass floor.

Down deep, drilled far into the planetary crust, a cavern opened out, a gaping shaft filled with a honeycomb of automated machinery and moving platforms and transport elevators and robotic handlers, all sliding and shifting in choreographed mechanical harmony.

"This is our main accumulation site," Sorz explained. "Raw ore from side shafts is brought here, then sorted and separated and routed to the various stages of processing. We can see some of those initial stages in the next building if you like. But of course the final processing stages are off limits to visitors, I'm afraid—partly because some of what we do is proprietary, but also because we're isolating 'strange matter' and working with magnetic monopoles, both of which are highly dangerous unless properly contained. So for your own safety this is as far as we can go."

Jeanne said to Gates, "We're kind of hitting a dead end here. I could use some good news."

"I'm still digging around in low-level systems, trying to locate anything about shipment scheduling or government contracts. Need a little more time."

Jeanne said out loud, "What exactly is 'strange matter,' and how does it come to be mined from a planet's crust?"

"Ah. Yes, it does sound rather like something made up, doesn't it. But it's very real. You can look it up."

"Just give me the abbreviated version."

"Well I'm no physicist, I only know what I've learned from the company. So bear with me. Strange matter is matter produced under extreme cosmic pressures, as in a neutron star or white dwarf star, or at the beginning of the universe. It contains a class of quarks known as strange quarks, as opposed to ordinary matter which has only up and down quarks." He chuckled. "You humans have such colorful names for these things: up, down, top, bottom, strange, charm—such an odd language, English. Anyway, most quark combinations are unstable and decay rather quickly, except for the up and down quarks of ordinary matter. However, under the right conditions, strange quark matter is, strangely, stable. Also heavy and dangerous."

"How dangerous?"

"Oh, not so bad as they used to think. At one time there was some worry that strange matter would convert any ordinary matter it touched into itself, and so wipe out everything it came into contact with."

"Oh my!"

"Fortunately that's not the case. Or I should say it can only happen if the strange matter is negatively charged, which would make it attract the positively charged nuclei of ordinary atoms—nuclei of course contain protons which are positively charged. However, if the strange matter itself is positively charged then it will repel ordinary nuclei and keep them apart. The latter turns out to be true, luckily for us. Or it may be that any negatively charged strange matter gets destroyed pretty quickly in nuclear reactions with other star stuff, sort of like matter-antimatter annihilation, leaving only the tamer positively charged variety for us to scoop up."

"That's a relief! But how does it get from a neutron star or white dwarf to this planet's crust."

"Well, it turns out Serebus IV is one of a few planets in any galaxy where a passing black hole happens to tear apart either a white dwarf or a neutron star—it occurs more often than you might think, especially in the denser and older parts of a galaxy—one went through this region only a couple hundred million years ago. The black hole's intense gravitational forces swirl that torn-off condensed matter around just outside its event horizon, generating incredible energy and magnetic fields and flinging out massive jets of exotic particles at nearly light-speed. Those exotic particles go on to seed any planets in nearby star systems. This is what we mine from deep in the planet's crust, where it finally gets stopped."

"I get it. I think. And that's why you set up on rocky hills and mountain sides, since that's where a planet's crust has buckled and been thrust up to the surface."

"Correct. Now what good is all that? Well, strange matter has very strange properties. It's reminiscent of the very first instants of the universe's birth when all quantum properties and forces were mixed together at the incredibly miniscule Planck scale, along with all the dimensions. Among other things that allows the existence of magnetic monopoles. Properly controlling strange matter let's us replicate some of those properties, like magnetic monopoles and mixed-up dimensions. With advanced technology to pry apart the core of the strange matter—sort of like splitting an atom, if I can use a very loose analogy—that then gives us access to the universe's curled up extra dimensions that exist at the sub-quantum Planck scale." He spread his paws. "But now you need a quantum-gravity theorist to explain how *that's* done. I'm afraid I've reached the limits of my comprehension."

"That's...more than I was expecting. Probably more than I needed to know."

Gates broke into her thoughts. "You were right about hitting a dead end. I need access to their shipping records. I can't get that here."

Jeanne faced Sorz. "This has been fascinating. But getting back to practicalities, it would be decidedly helpful if we could see your actual shipping facility."

"Um, that's not usually part of the tour...."

"But you can make an exception, right? The Spraang need to know that you can fill their increased shipment orders while still keeping up with your normal output."

"I see. Well, I suppose that's reasonable. All right, I'll just redirect our personnel carrier here for a detour before we return to the offices." He made a manual adjustment to the carrier's controls and the little transport veered off toward a side exit. "We'll have to go around the other factory modules, those final processing stages I talked about, and reach the shipping depot from outside."

The carrier took them through the side exit. They left the factory and Sorz drove them by hand along a paved access lot that curved past more factory modules, over the hilltop and down the other side, finally arriving at the last module sitting on a broad plateau cut into the rock. A single transport container rested on the plateau, backed up to the module's open loading dock.

Sorz stopped at another side entrance and led everyone inside. His voice echoed in the hollow and relatively quiet interior. "This is our shipping warehouse." He indicated the many specially-shielded containers neatly stacked, shipping labels and *"Extreme Danger—Not Kidding!"* warnings slapped on their sides, ready for pickup, several being loaded just now through the open loading dock into the transport outside.

"Gates?" Jeanne inquired in her head.

"No go. Being blocked strongly here. It's that Agency-style security firewall again. Looks like Leonore didn't want anyone finding out where her shipment went."

"Agh! All right, hold on. Let me try something." She made a show of assessing the warehouse space with her eyes, walking a few paces this way and that. Finally she turned back to Sorz. "Adequate, I suppose. But is this a typical day? I'd like to get a look at your recent shipping schedule, so we have a better idea of the kind of logistics we're up against on more of a regular basis."

Sorz lifted his rodent eyebrows. "Uh, that's highly irregular. I'm sure you appreciate that we need to keep the details of our operations confidential from other companies like ours, who would love any intel on how we do things and who we do it with, maybe even to poach from our customer base."

Jeanne put on her most serious look of disappointment—which didn't take much play-acting just then.

Apparently Sorz was familiar enough with human emotions to read disapproval in her expression. He twitched his whiskers, said quickly, "But perhaps I can let you have a just a glimpse, eyes only, no copies to take with you. Would that be acceptable?"

"Let's try it and see."

Sorz moved to a control panel, typed in a personal username, then a lengthy password, stepped through three-factor authentication, waited while he received a one-time verification code through his cyber-neural comms, entered that, checked the "I am not an AI" box, selected "all images with bridges and sleeping kittens" in the thumbnail picture gallery, pressed his paw to the screen and his face to the camera—then had to do it all over again since he had mixed up his work password with a private one.

Finally the screen agreed that he was he and rewarded him with a list of the latest month's outgoing shipments.

Jeanne leaned close for a look. Sure enough, an extra large government consignment had gone out just that morning, picked up by Q-Haul, the Quantum Haulers do-it-yourself rocket rental company, for transfer to one of their cargo vessels at the space port.

Figures. Leonore wouldn't trust a standard shipping line, but would have some private guys hire a truck and move it themselves.

She sighed. "Thank you, Sorz. We have all we need." In her head she said, "Back to the space port, Gates. Looks like you're going to have to hack into ship departures."

Chapter 5

After their tour Sorz drove them back to the front offices. Jeanne made their excuses, claiming a pressing need to make a diplomatic appointment and apologizing for not sticking around to discuss business arrangements in more depth, as Sorz obviously expected. They departed hastily in the autocab that had brought them, leaving the company rep standing on his office building's doorstep mystified and more than a little frustrated.

As he dwindled in the rear-view, Roingroing finally spoke. "Asss you requessssted I have ssstayed sssilent thisss whole time. But I mussst confesss I found sssome of your wordsss puzzling. Many of your ssstatementsss ssseemed, imposssibly, not to match reality."

"Yeah, that's the subterfuge part. I don't expect you to get it."

"Well, I cannot dissspute the resssultsss."

"Funny how that works, huh?"

They continued on into town and the space port. Once through customs, Gates found the flow of cyber data much more accessible, at least to him with his super-classified Agency spy software. The landing field kept scrupulous records of freighter arrivals and departures (unlike the comings and goings of living and procreating beings, ships were far fewer and much easier to keep track of). It didn't take long for Gates to determine that the local Q-Haul shipment had been transferred to a larger Q-Haul cargo vessel, which then departed for a destination star listed as XR-10937a.

"Got it!" Gates announced as they walked (and bounced) through the small-craft terminal on the way to Roingroing's courier ship. "It's an out-of-the-way star, a big one, with small rocky planets, none of them habitable."

"How big a star?" Jeanne asked with apprehension.

"Very. More than a hundred solar masses."

Jeanne sucked in a breath. "That's what she needs to deploy her weapon! We've got to get there first, stop it before it's fully assembled! Roingroing," she said aloud, "we've got the coordinates. We need to jet, beat Leonore to the punch!"

"I don't undersssssta...."

"It means no time to spare. Let's get going, fast!"

They hailed a field robo-transport and rode back to the Spraang courier craft. At Jeanne's insistence, and against his inbuilt inclination, Roingroing violated normal traffic protocols and cut in ahead of several other small craft riding up the magnetic lift beam.

Once in space, and ignoring angry orders from ground control to return at once, Jeanne gave Roingroing the coordinates. He fed them into his nav system, waited anxious seconds while the computer compensated for any anomalies or other dangers along the way, then engaged his sub-quantum FTL drive. The little ship shivered and fell into superposed sub-quantum dimensional space.

* * * *

This time the trip took longer, long enough for an impromptu bull session while enroute.

Jeanne, squished awkwardly into her Spraang-designed cushion, felt pressured—physically as well as intellectually—to ask a question that had long bothered her. "Say, do either of you know why we don't feel these curled-up compressed dimensions when we make these jumps? Or get curled up and compressed ourselves?"

"Esssentially we do," Roingroing offered. "It'sss jussst that whatever dimensssion we happen to be in alwaysss appearsss infinite in exssstent when we're inssside it. It'sss only to outssside obssserversss that a dimensssion appearsss curled up. Ssso everything alwaysss ssseemsss normal to usss. It'sss all relative."

"Uh...I'll take your word for it. Quantum relativity gives me a headache. As long as it works. Not that it makes me feel a whole lot better." She had a sudden thought. "Hey wait. Does that mean our ordinary three-dimensional space could actually be curled up inside some higher dimension, and we wouldn't know it?"

"That isss correct. It'sss the reassson we can entangle all dimensssionsss with ours and come out pretty much anyplacssse we choossse."

Jeanne swallowed. "That's...a little disconcerting." She made an effort to shake off the counterintuitive and highly unnerving notion. "But back to more immediate concerns." She switched to her private comm, asked, "Gates, how long ago did the Q-Haul leave?"

"Not quite two hours before us."

"Roingroing," she said aloud, "can you bring us out of FTL drive two light-hours distant from the Q-Haul's destination coordinates?"

"Yesss. Commercsssial carriersss mussst file a precissse flight plan, ssso I can plot a ssspecific finisssh point. But why two light-hoursss?"

"They left two hours ahead of us."

"Ah, I sssee. If we ssstop two light-hoursss away, EM emisssionsss from the Q-Haul'sss arrival will jussst be reaching usss then."

"Right. But our emissions won't get to them for another

two hours, so we're safe from detection. The question is, can we see them from that far away?"

"Visssually, no, even usssing my bessst magnification. However, commercsssial carriersss mussst transsssmit a transssponder sssignal, one that is almossst impossssible to disssable."

"And since Leonore thinks she got her shipment out without being noticed, she probably won't even try disabling it. Especially since doing so would draw unneeded attention from the Q-Haul company and their insurance carrier, if nothing else. Good. Her attempt at cleverness might just be her undoing. Okay, find that transponder signal as soon as we arrive. And keep a close watch on it. We need to know exactly where they go in this star system."

"That will be ssssoon. Ssshutting down sssub-quantum drive in three, two, one—"

The computer timed their dimensional return to the picosecond. Ahead, a massive blue-white giant star burst into being as a small glaringly brilliant disc, its light filtered down through the view port to levels tolerable to organic lifeforms but still pouring out unrelenting and deadly hard radiation in the invisible spectrum. The courier craft maintained just enough local dimensional warping and magnetic field generation to deflect that radiation around itself.

"Adjusssting sssenssssorsss for interferencssse and sssolar ssstatic." Roingroing's pseudopods played over his controls. The nav plot on the view window expanded and cleared to show this star system in miniature. "There'sss the transssponder."

On the screen a small green dot appeared about fourteen AU's closer in, and beside it an ID tag that identified the ship and its registration, along with an attached marketing slogan in Galactic Trade Standard that said: "Q-Haul—We move the universe!"

Roingroing fine-tuned his equipment to filter out more of the star's interference. "There'sss another sssignal." He pointed a pseudopod at a spot on the screen just ahead of the moving Q-Haul dot.

"Another transponder?"

"No, thisss isss weak, almossst lossst in the ssstatic. It'sss jussst ssstandard background emisssionsss from another ssship. No—two ssshipsss, clossse together."

"And the transponder is moving toward them. It's a rendezvous. That's where they're assembling the weapon! We need to get in there."

"Are you sssure? I ssshould advissse you that my vesssel hasss no weaponsss."

"That's just as well. I don't think we want to blow up a massive strange-matter doomsday device anyway. Who knows what that might do? We just need to stop it from being completed and deployed."

"Jussst usss?" Roingroing trembled a little.

"No, just me. You two will have to stay here."

"That doesss not ssseem like a sssound ssstrategy!"

"Trust me, this is what I do. How close can you jump us in to that Q-Haul?"

"Asssuming they sssusssstain a sssteady orbit, asss clossse asss you wisssh."

"Good. Put us right behind them. If I remember right, those rentals all have an emergency rescue hatch on top."

"Yesss. But my ssship hasss no docking port. And we have no ssspace sssuitsss if you expect to go outssside."

"Leave that to me. You do have an emergency airlock or escape mechanism?"

"Jussst the main door. But when usssed in ssspace a

membrane ssseals it off from the ssship's interior ssso it actsss asss one of your human airlocksss."

"That'll work. Um, how soon do you think before they discover us, once we get there?"

"My ssship can mimic thisss ssstar'sss energy patternsss and re-transsssmit them, make usss ssseem to be part of the ssstatic—if no one looksss too clossssely. That ssshould gain usss a little time, though minutesss at mossst."

"We'll have to act quickly then. All right, let's do it. Jump us in."

"If you insssisssst. Jussst remember when we get there, they are actually two hoursss ahead of when we're ssseeing them now." He turned back to his control panel to input the nav instructions.

Gates spoke up in her head. "Is this smart? I'm kind of with Roingroing on this one."

"It has to be done, Gates. You know that."

"Wish I was coming with you."

"Me too. But you be a good watchdog and hold down the fort here. And keep Roingroing calm." She activated her Astra Woman rejuvenation and sens-suit, this time with the addition of a space-vacuum survival feature.

As the suit tightened around her its nano particles interlocked to form an airtight barrier, at the same time selectively pulling in oxygen from the air while breaking down her CO_2 exhalations into their component molecules, scrubbing the carbon and re-using the O_2. The neck of her suit extended up to form a transparent bubble just slightly larger than her head.

She felt in back for her carry pack, made sure she still had the shadow cloak.

The courier craft shimmied as Roingroing made his jump. And now abruptly ahead of them, a couple of ship lengths away, the Q-Haul hovered in garish two-toned maroon and cream colors, its "We move the universe" company motto plastered on its side.

Beyond it another larger ship loomed like a bulky asteroid, it's black hull clunky and ugly. The two appeared to be docked together, side-to-side. The third ship they had detected must be out of sight behind these two.

Roingroing piloted them up and over so the courier ship would shield the Q-Haul's emergency rescue hatch from the sun's lethal radiations.

"I ssstill don't sssee how...." He stopped short as he swiveled around and caught sight of Jeanne's transformed youthful appearance and sleek sens-suit. "Thisss isss sssurprisssing!"

She grinned and gave a thumbs-up. "Welcome to my side hustle! Now as soon as I get into the rescue hatch you jump back out to a safe distance. Don't want you to be spotted and captured or anything. Just don't go too far in case I need to call you back here in a hurry." She scooched out of her cushion-seat, unkinking her cramped limbs with considerable relief, tried not to hit her head on the low cabin ceiling, and moved the few inches to the side door.

The Braille-like controls there seemed simple enough: two bumps, one no doubt for open, one for close. She tried the top one.

A flexible but tough pinkish membrane descended around her, sealing itself against walls and floor. A warning light flashed, a series of loud squeaks and whistles in the Spraang native language sounded an alert, then the membrane bowed inward as the ship evacuated air from this cocoon-like "airlock." Finally the outer door slid open and she faced the vacuum of raw space.

A few meters in front of her the Q-Haul's emergency

hatch drifted, looking small and out of reach, and just beyond it the infinite depths of empty space—cold, merciless and bottomless. It reminded her a little too much of leaping onto that hotel balcony.

"Gates," she said on their private comms. "Once you jump away we'll be out of personal comm range. If I'm successful here I'll try to get to this ship's trans-space communicator and contact you guys that way for pick up. If not I'll find some other way to signal you. Or if things go wrong and I don't make it back—"

"Don't say that!"

"If I don't make it back, you be nice to your new master— I mean partner—"

"Stop saying that!"

"And be sure to go outside when you need to pee, and remember to wipe your feet when you go back inside, and don't bite anybody unless they really really deserve it."

"I'm not listening!"

"Yes you are. You're my good boy, Gates, always."

Well. Now or never. She held her breath (again unnecessarily), took careful aim and pushed off.

She banged into the Q-Haul's hull thankfully close to target, grabbed a handhold and steadied herself over the hatch. The access controls had been designed for universal rescue by any species, and since this was a commercial vehicle for general public hire security hadn't been a big consideration. It took only a few seconds to get the hatch open and float in feet-first. As she did so Roingroing's courier ship began moving away, Gates at the forward view port looking forlornly out at her—then it visually wavered as it dimensionally transitioned, leaving only a gaping void where it had been.

Feeling suddenly alone, Jeanne sealed the hatch behind

her and cycled atmosphere into the small airlock. She reached around into her carry pack and pulled out the shadow cloak. But in weightlessness it didn't want to cooperate, flopping around as she tried to fit it over herself. And despite all efforts her feet stuck out—without gravity the cloth had no weight to pull it down. Oh well, she'd have to make do.

Now would anyone be waiting on the other side of the airlock's inner door? Her Astra Woman enhanced strength and sens-suit prepared her for most confrontations, but better if the crew had left the ship. They should have—who would want to sit in a truck for two hours after unloading?

Pressure equalized and the inner door opened. So far no welcoming committee, just a passage between the cargo hold and the pilot compartment. Her sens-suit detected no movement, no sound or heat sources other than normal ship machinery. And the six couches up front were unoccupied. She retracted her suit's helmet and floated further in, down the passage and through the cargo hold—empty and smelling of dry synthetic packing materials. The docking door to the larger attached ship stood open, exposing a broad well-lit loading corridor on the far side ending in an interior transport elevator. The shipment of concentrated strange matter must have gone through there to somewhere else in the big ship.

She pulled herself along toward the transport elevator. Now where would a deranged, megalomanic mass-murderer be assembling a strange matter weapon? The Gu'gundreans had described it as pretty large. It would need a big compartment, maybe with a door to the outside. Say, a shuttle bay.

Luckily major ships like this had colorful deck schematics posted everywhere, like the one right beside the elevator door. Yup, shuttle bay, two decks down, then straight ahead.

She decided against calling for the transport elevator. Might attract attention, and so far she still appeared to have the element of surprise. She opted for the personnel companionway next to it, poked her head warily into the open shaft.

No one in sight, just a steeply-angled ship's ladder, some basic lighting, electrical conduits and a few pipes, all a cheerless dull gray with white handrails and trim. She floated down the two levels to the deck she wanted, peeked out of the open hatch there.

A long empty corridor stretched before her. All right, now where were the crew? This didn't seem normal. A ship of this size generally carried a pretty large complement.

Then again, Leonore might want to keep everyone involved in her project to a bare minimum. So maybe it made sense that she'd send this ship out with only a skeleton crew.

She tucked the shadow cloak close around her and shoved off into the corridor.

She'd made it about half way when a figure finally appeared from a side room: a toadie in black combat gear. Jeanne held herself and the shadow cloak as still as possible while gliding weightless toward the overly-muscled mercenary, and began looking hastily for something to grab onto to stop her progress.

But she had unwisely aimed herself right down this wide corridor's middle. She wondered fleetingly why her sens-suit didn't come equipped with a jet pack. Sounded like a good idea right about now. She'd have to bring that up with her Agency if she ever got back in good standing with them. Or ever got back.

The toadie still hadn't seen her when she crashed into

him full bore. He jerked in utter surprise, then immediately went into defensive battle mode.

But in weightlessness his muscles proved less effective than he might have liked. Jeanne managed to push off from him while he flailed and grasped for his nearly-invisible attacker, and their mutual momentum sent them flying apart.

Jeanne got a purchase on a wall handhold, then quickly swung further along the corridor. Behind her the toadie struggled to right himself and regain stability.

Up ahead she could hear a scuffle of bodies coming from an intersecting passageway. Her sens-suit's fine-detail sensors distinguished half a dozen individuals. The toadie she'd run into must have called for reinforcements using a private combat circuit.

This time she kept close enough to the wall that she could easily stop herself and go immobile. The shadow cloak settled down just as the six new toadie troops came around the corner—awkwardly, piling into one another and banging against the bulkhead as they tried to negotiate the sharp turn. It seemed they weren't all that used to working in weightlessness either.

They spread out now along the corridor, looking for the intruder they expected to find. The toadie she'd had the fender-bender with started yelling and pointing in her direction. She looked down. Her feet! Curse her long legs.

She triggered another mental code in her cyber-neural net, one not often used since it had detrimental side-effects, setting her internal nano-particles to work on her sympathetic nervous system, speeding up her reflexes and her sense of time passage. Instantly she seemed to see everything in slow motion. In this accelerated subjective-time state she launched herself at an angle toward the opposite wall between the nearest two toadies, caught one by the arm and swiveled around him as if he were a pole, using her feet to carom off the wall and redirect her angular momentum further down the corridor.

The next toadie tracked her cloak's visible distortion in the air—and probably her feet, too—reached out and grabbed for her as she passed. She batted the arm away but not before he got a fistful of cloak. It slipped off in his hand as she flew on by.

Only one more of these guys to go between her and the shuttle bay. So far she'd taken them all by surprise with her speeded-up reaction time and that handy-dandy bit of techno-camo—she really regretted losing that. But now the last toadie could see her plainly, and he'd had time to draw his zapper pistol. It swung in a seemingly slowed-down arc toward her.

She banked off another wall and kicked hard, curled herself into a ball and aimed right for the gun-toting toad. Just before reaching him she straightened out feet first, deflecting his gun arm with one foot and clipping him in the chin with the other—guess her feet were good for something after all. With her quickened reaction time she managed to snatch the gun out of his hand as he flipped over backward and spun in the air before fetching up against the doorway to another side room.

Still in accelerated subjective time Jeanne pivoted off another handhold and propelled herself the rest of the way to the shuttle bay entrance while the toadies were still trying to figure out what had just happened. She arrested her forward motion against the shuttle bay bulkhead, aimed the zapper pistol at the door's locking mechanism, set it for maximum, and fired.

The electrical plasma discharge crackled and sizzled

against metal, throwing off white-hot sparks and bitter metallic-ozone smoke. The door jarred open a crack. She grabbed the edge and forced it the rest of the way with her enhanced sens-suit strength, slipped through quickly and off to the side, out of line-of-fire of the toadies behind her.

And now she stopped while the hackles rose on her neck. In the middle of the hollow shuttle bay a dark spherical polyhedron at least twice her own height floated in a magnetic containment field, rotating slowly in the weightless environment, accompanied by a low power hum. It evoked in her an ominous sense of foreboding.

"Jeanne!" The voice came from a holo projection of a figure standing near the sphere: a woman of extended years with wavy gray hair, dressed in robes of the Council of Goodwill, the white robes of Senior Councilor Leonore Squag to be exact. The apparition smiled expansively. "You continue to surprise. Well done for getting here! Maybe I underestimated you. No matter, you're just a smidgeon too late. As you see, the weapon is finished and ready to deploy."

At that moment the troop of toadies stuck their angry heads and raised guns in. Leonore waved them back. "No, no need for that now. Let's be civil. In fact, I find it fitting that you should be here, Jeanne, to witness this moment."

Jeanne slowed her time sense to normal. "Don't gloat, Leonore. I'm a little surprised to see you, too, even by holo projection. Sub-quantum trans-space communication is expensive. You must be pretty sure of yourself to use it to oversee things personally."

"Yes, well you know what they say: if you want something done right...."

Jeanne gestured at the hovering sphere. "That's quite a paper weight. Is that thing made entirely of strange matter?"

"Pretty near."

"There must be enough there to supply a thousand FTL ships!"

"More than that."

Jeanne snatched up one of the worker's tethers conveniently placed around the shuttle bay and pushed off cautiously toward the sphere.

"I wouldn't get too close," Leonore advised. "Negatively charged strange matter. Touch it and you'll be absorbed and disappear into non-dimensional non-space."

Jeanne tugged on the tether to halt her progress. "Negatively charged? I thought all strange matter we mine is positively charged so it repels ordinary matter. I don't see how it can collapse a star, let alone a whole galaxy."

"You're quite right. But it turns out we can convert one kind of strange matter into the other, with the right nuclear reactions. You see, any matter particle—a proton or neutron—is made up of three quarks, each having a positive or negative partial charge, adding up to one full charge. I won't bore you with the details, but it's possible to change strange matter's combination of quarks around so its particles have a net negative charge, just as we can change a positively charged proton into a negatively charged anti-proton and create antimatter. I suppose you might call this anti-strange-matter. And like antimatter, it can only be made in small amounts and has to be held in a magnetic containment field."

"So, what then? You just launch it into a star like this one?"

"Oh, no. That would merely collapse the star and turn it into a black hole. That won't affect the rest of the galaxy any more than any other black hole does—which would be a pointless waste of perfectly good strange matter. No, it has to be carried in on a ship like this one, so that the ship's sub-quantum FTL drive, while it's still running, quantumly entangles all dimensions in the interior of the star. At that point we switch off the weapon's magnetic containment field, and those two processes working together—or in opposition, I forget which—will both attract all nearby ordinary matter into the strange matter while at the same time collapsing all dimensions in on themselves. Once that begins, the super-massive star and its existing gravitational attraction to other stars serves as a critical starter mass, creating a runaway chain reaction that eventually consumes the entire galaxy."

"That's evil—diabolical, insane!"

"Or is it genius? Maybe even destiny? Remember, peace through fear—the only way to truly secure the future of the universe for all sentient creatures. Well, all of them not caught in the chain reaction, that is."

Jeanne didn't know what to say. "How do I know you've actually done it? That this sphere is what you claim it is?"

"Ah, you need a demonstration." She pointed at a toadie. "You, toss one of those cargo hooks at the sphere."

The toadie obediently detached a metal hook from its holder on a bulkhead, threw it toward the sphere. It sped up in mid-flight and snapped onto the sphere's surface as if magnetized, then immediately sank inward while disintegrating and converting to brilliant light energy.

Jeanne watched in morbid fascination and growing revulsion. "So that's it? You're just going to destroy our galaxy for your own power and ego?"

"What? Of course not! I'm not a monster. Just a pragmatist. I'll give the governments every opportunity to see reason, to work together with me to establish peaceful rule. I'm merely going to deploy the weapon in tight orbit around this star, ready to drop at my command. It's the ultimate deterrent." She shrugged. "On the other hand, I have to consider the greater good. If one galaxy has to perish so others will flourish, so be it. I can live with that."

"Unlike all the people in the galaxy! And you say you're not a monster."

"Po-*ta*-to, po-*tah*-to. You do realize this is all your fault, Jeanne."

"*My* fault?"

"Until you butted in, the whole Plan—the demonstrations of the weapon, the ultimatums to the various governments—could be anonymous, no one had to know who was orchestrating it all. So it could play out gradually, progressively, more tactfully, not so harshly. But because you discovered who was actually behind everything I had to step up my timetable. No more warnings. I had to make the threat real and immediate."

Jeanne looked at the humming and slowly rotating massive sphere. "Yeah, I'd say this is pretty immediate."

"So you see, whatever actual danger the galaxy is in, it's entirely on you."

"That's pretty twisted logic!"

"Mmm, pragmatic logic."

"Hold on, something's not quite right here. I thought your Plan hinged on you attaining immortality from the Gu'gundreans?"

"Well, that's ideal, certainly. And I still hope to get the secret from them at some point, one way or another. But now I've decided—for pragmatic reasons—that it's not absolutely essential. Or I should say your interference decided it for me. You've been such a pain in my side. But no matter. It's the greater good again. You see, while I may be the best one for the job, in the larger scheme of things others of similar mind and resolve could take over if needed. I've gathered a trusted coterie of lieutenants who believe as I do, and who've vowed to carry on the work, our grand vision for the universe. So even if I don't live on I've set things up so my legacy will."

"Lieutenants who believe as you do—you mean who you've brainwashed into believing!"

"That's very cynical. It's just a slight surgical alteration to their cyber-neural implants to ensure their loyalty to me—can't have them going off-script. But I prefer to see us as an enlightened few, a select circle of far-seeing visionaries, the only ones with the foresight and courage to do what has to be done. And in the end it's not even me or those lieutenants who matter. It's that work, that vision, that is truly important."

Jeanne shook her head, at a loss.

Leonore smiled a self-satisfied smile. "But now my people will be leaving. Your timing was perfect, if futile. You arrived right as we were wrapping things up. The cargo truck that brought the strange matter is undocking and heading for its home base as we speak. The scientists who converted that shipment into my weapon are already on board the small transport ship I've provided for them. My private guard are on their way to join them. You, I'm afraid, will be staying here. Can't have you interfering in my plans any further."

Jeanne looked around. Sure enough, the toadies had all left.

Leonore turned to go. "Oh, and just so you know, no one can stop me now. If anyone—including you—tries to attack this ship or change its nav programming, or disable any part of the weapon, it deploys automatically. Well, okay then... have fun while you can!" Her hologram image winked out.

Jeanne floated there stunned, nothing but the deep hum

of the strange matter sphere to break the silence. She increased her suit's sensitivity, but detected no other lifeforms in the vicinity.

And that sphere—she had no delusions of trying to deactivate it. Leonore would have made sure it couldn't be interfered with. Besides which, Jeanne's knowledge of quantum physics wasn't exactly up to meddling with something that advanced and super-dangerous, even if she had the tools to do so, which she didn't see any sign of lying around. The scientists probably took all that with them.

She turned and exited the shuttle bay, found another deck schematic, then made her way forward through several connecting corridors and up four levels to the ship's bridge. She encountered no one on the way. She really was alone.

The bridge seemed inordinately small for so large a ship: four acceleration couches facing a control consol that curved around below a panoramic view port. Out the window stars peppered a black sky, while this system's sun glared intensely off to the side, even dimmed down through many levels of filtering.

She moved to the consol, looking for the sub-quantum trans-space communicator.

Found it. Sabotaged—ripped out completely, nothing but a vacant hole in the panel. So much for calling for help.

Now what? She couldn't try moving the ship. Leonore's warning had to be taken seriously.

From the corner of her eye she noticed the stars out the forward view port shifting, sliding off to one side while the sun rotated around to end up almost dead center. She heard the low whine of the ship's FTL drive warming up. Must be an automatic program Leonore had left behind, the next step in her unspeakable Plan.

Abruptly she felt the familiar shiver of dimensional

transition. The ship jumped—

And came out right next to the sun.

Right next to it! When Leonore had said a tight orbit she hadn't been exaggerating. The ship was actually orbiting inside the star's corona, only its sub-quantum dimensional field keeping it from being incinerated in the unimaginably intense heat and energetic solar ejecta. Leonore must figure hiding in the star's brilliance would make it harder to detect or to safely approach, but this was madness!

At least the ship sheltered her for the moment—as long as they kept the engine running.

Had Leonore accounted for that? For fuel depletion and orbital decay from friction with coronal particles? She would have to, if she wanted her long-range plans to work. Or had she gone truly mad? What would happen if something went wrong and the ship fell in unintentionally, by accident?

While Jeanne mulled these unpalatable scenarios, a faint crackle came from the private comm channel in her head. Then a broken voice: "Jean...hear me?...respond...can you...?"

For a second she thought she was hearing the Gu'gundreans again through her defective translator. Then she realized it had to be Gates. "Gates! Where are you?"

"Jeanne! I hear you now. We're coming up in the shadow cast by your ship—we tracked your jump. Get to an escape hatch on the starboard side."

"No, you shouldn't be here! The sun's corona will boil that little courier craft like an egg."

"The shadow's protecting us, for a few minutes at least. Don't waste time arguing. Move!"

Jeanne headed out the rear of the control room, hurriedly scanned a deck schematic for starboard side escape hatches, then kicked off, flying down corridors and companionways, bouncing off walls, finally braking hard against the outer hull where big red letters said "Emergency Exit—Thanks For Flying With Us, and don't forget to leave a review!" next to a smiley face and a thumbs-up. She put her fist through the smiley face to break the safety seal on the airlock, quickly opened the door and entered, reactivating her suit's bubble helmet and space-vacuum survival feature as she went.

"Gates, are you there?" She started cycling air from the airlock. "I'm in the forward-most starboard escape hatch."

"Got it. Moving up to it now."

"How are we doing this?"

"Jump. Just like you did the first time."

"We're inside the star's corona! It's mighty hot out there."

"We'll get as close as possible. And both ships are maintaining enough dimensional warping and magnetic field generation to shield themselves from this extreme environment. That should extend to the space between them too, somewhat."

"*Somewhat?* Love the confidence! Wait, speaking of dimensional warping, won't that just repel the two ships' masses, push them apart?"

"Roingroing's working on a way around that, by rapidly cycling the frequency of his ship's field, sort of switching it in and out of phase with your ship's field many times per second. That should let us squeeze in further. Full disclosure, it might make for a rough ride for you, though."

"Yeah, what else is new? Let's just do it."

"Okay. We're at the hatch, pressing in closer...getting some vibration...we're about at our limit. Ready when you are."

Jeanne popped the outer hatch. Charged particles from the sun's corona danced like an aurora borealis around the rim, leaked in and ran up and down her limbs in static electrical surges that stabbed at her even through her suit. She wondered what it would be like if these ships weren't shielding her. Already she could feel her body temperature rising.

The courier craft hung off in space farther away than she'd hoped, about three times more than before. Its little side door looked awfully small. She put that out of her mind, braced herself, took *extra* careful aim, and shoved.

The coronal particles bombarded her in waves out here, and the heat engulfed her like a superheated dry sauna. Her suit compensated as best it could, though she felt she'd cook if this went on another two seconds.

But what really discombobulated her was the vibration. It started as a discomfiting pulsation, grew into an annoying tremor, then escalated to a violent shaking. That must be Roingroing's rapid dimensional frequency cycling. Well, Gates had warned her of a rough ride.

Just when she thought she couldn't take any more the door to Roingroing's ship swelled in front of her. She caught its edge, pulled herself inside with a final superhuman effort and hit the "close" button.

The vibration trailed off. She sagged against the membrane inside the airlock. How wonderful to be free of that intolerable shaking—and from the heat and everything else!

She slumped in exhaustion as she felt the ship quiver, fold all dimensions in on itself and make its leap out of there.

Chapter 6

She caught only fragments after that: the membrane retracting, her being laid out where two of the ship's cushions had been removed—much more comfortable than trying to scrunch into one of those unappealing little things—Gates firmly telling her to reverse her rejuvenation *now!*

Good advice, because she really felt drained. Between using her rejuvenation for that long, plus her artificially speeded-up time sense, not to mention just standard adrenaline crash after an extended, intense life-or-death close call, she needed about a week's sleep.

And food. Visions of hot chicken enchiladas smothered in melted mozzarella cheese swam in her head—yes, that again; her imagination seemed too tired to dream up anything new. Except maybe the melted mozzarella part.

She drifted off to sleep, only awakening briefly when the ship swerved and rocked gently as it entered a magnetic descent corridor, getting a glimpse of the city of Lusteer out the view port, then being vaguely aware of landing in the Spraang consulate garage.

In her half-awake state she felt little elf fingers lift her tenderly and carry her out of the ship—no, those were pseudopods, surprisingly soft. Several Spraang had formed a carry brigade on each side of her, their thoughtfully diminutive bounces smoothed out by the rubber-band-like pseudopod arms—or tentacles, or spaghetti noodles, she wasn't sure what to call them.

Rather soothing, like being rocked in a cradle, she decided as she drifted off again. Nice little elves.

* * * *

The next thing she knew she awoke in her visitor's bungalow, more or less alert but groggy. And starving. And worried.

Super worried, now that memory came flooding back. She sat up. "Gates!"

Immediately he ran in through the open door, started licking her face. "You're okay!"

"Good to see you, too. Now cut it out."

He controlled himself. "You had us really concerned. You were out for three days."

"Three *days!*"

"The Spraang managed to give you some kind of intravenous nutrients so you wouldn't be too deprived."

"Yeah, tell that to my stomach." She clamped a hand over her growling abdomen, got stiffly to her feet while trying to work out a kink in her side and another one in her neck. "Look, do we know what Leonore's been up to?"

"That's a question Roingroing and I have both been asking."

"I'd like to see him, get his take on it. Do we know where he is right now?"

"On his way to his meditation dome. He says he'll meet us there."

"He does? How do you know?"

"I just talked to him."

Jeanne shot Gates a sharp look. "You just *talked to him!?*"

"Uh, that may take a little explaining. Maybe we should discuss this after we're all together."

"Good idea. I'd like to hear that explanation! And call up the kitchen on the way, order us something to eat. Not chicken, though, I think I'm over that."

They made the short walk through the alien's exotic and fragrant garden to the meditation dome, found Roingroing waiting when they entered.

"Okay, spill it," Jeanne demanded. "What's up with you two?"

"Nicssse to sssee you've sssurvived," Roingroing said. "What do you wisssh usss to ssspill?"

"I mean, there's something weird going on between the two of you, and I want to know what it is right now."

"I asssume you mean our new ability to converssse."

"So it's true? Gates talked to you?"

"Yesss."

Gates said, "When you didn't contact us, and we saw those two ships leaving, then the one you were on jumped in next to the sun, that seemed like a pretty good signal that you needed our help. I had to find a way to communicate with Roingroing."

"He sssurprisssed me. But mosssst usssefully."

Jeanne raised an eyebrow. "Oh, you're hearing him right now? Fascinating. Go on."

Gates looked sheepish. "It was an urgent and exceedingly desperate situation. I suppose that extra-motivated me. And since he'd already seen you in your rejuvenated Astra Woman state, I kind of felt I had an excuse. At any rate, I figured out how to bypass my own security protocols and link into his cyber-neural comm so I could talk directly with him like I do with you."

"That's not supposed to be possible!" Jeanne looked flabbergasted.

"You know how good I am at hacking into things. This

time I sort of hacked my own cyber systems. It never occurred to me to do that before, for some reason. But it actually wasn't all that different from hacking anything else."

Jeanne chortled. "That's amazing! And hilarious. I can't imagine what the guys back at the Agency might say about it. But it does explain how you two could work together to pull me out of that sticky predicament. That had to take some skillful coordination. I kind of wondered about that in the back of my mind at the time, but it wasn't a big priority then." She adjusted her mind-set to this new concept. "So Roingroing, now you know about our secret Agency undercover work."

"Jusssst the basssicsss. I'm sssure you'll fill me in on the ressst asss we go."

"About that," Gates put in, "I realize I violated our Agency oaths, and several espionage acts."

"Well, I forgive you. And I think our oath to protect the galaxy takes precedence over our oath to any law and intelligence organization. Besides, it seems to me the Council and maybe even the Agency have already violated a lot more than just their oaths. Anyway, you're not the only one who gave away our secret identities. I may have already revealed my Astra Woman alter ego to someone else."

"Really? Who?"

"Remember our flitty-flyer pilot, Trix? When she flew me up to our hotel room balcony so I could retrieve my goo suit, she saw me transform just before I went in. Couldn't avoid it. She doesn't know much more than that yet, but she's pretty sharp. She'll put a few things together."

Gates shook his head. "What are we, telling the whole galaxy now?"

"Let's not go that far. Although...." A half-formed thought

tickled the back of her mind. "You know, telling the right people actually might not be a bad idea."

"Oh-oh. You've got a crazy look. What are you thinking now?"

"Not sure yet, just one of those elusive ideas that won't quite gel. Let me stew on it. Speaking of stew, where's our food?"

"Ssshould we not dissscuss Leonore's recsssent activitiesss?"

"You're right. Stomach, behave yourself! So what's our un-favorite Senior Councilor been up to while I've been asleep?"

"More than we'd like," Gates said. "Roingroing's high-level confidential connections have been chattering like crazy."

"So we still have an ear through the consulate's channels, then. That's good."

"My sssourcesss tell me ssshe hasss delivered another more ssseriousss ultimatum to the governmentsss. And ssshe hasss given them jussst one week to sssubmit or ssshe will ssset off her weapon."

"A week? Wow! And I just slept through the first three days of it? That's not good. What about the governments? What are they planning to do about it?"

"They are in chaosss and disssagreement. There's no consssensssusss, jussst disssorganized ideasss."

"Yeah. Getting a bunch of planetary governments to work together is a dicey proposition in the best of times. I can't imagine what wrench this has thrown into the gears. Sorry, Roingroing, that's another metaphor I don't feel like explaining right now."

Gates said, "So at this point no one knows where Leonore is. Once she finalized her weapon she went off the grid. She could be anywhere, inside the galaxy or out of it. Speculation is that she's still here inside our galaxy, though, because sub-quantum trans-space communication starts to acquire significant delay over intergalactic distances. The analysts think she needs to maintain a close watch on things, along with the ability to communicate with the governments in real time. Also to be able to trigger the weapon at a moment's notice if it comes to that. So they think she's most likely still somewhere reasonably close by, and within easy communication range of a major political hub."

"Like Lusteer."

"That's one theory."

"It's a good one." Jeanne pondered. "My feeling is she never really left. She supervised her weapon deployment by holo projection, which she could easily do from here. And Gates you said the signals for her original weapons tests were traced back here, too. I suspect she has a secret base of operations somewhere right here in this city. In fact, I'm beginning to think this has been her whole center of operations all along."

"How doesss that make sssenssse? If ssshe doesss dessstroy the galaxy, won't ssshe be caught up in it?"

"Well, she's not suicidal. She intends to rule. She probably plans to leave in a private ship at the last minute. From her two weapon demonstrations we know it takes a couple of weeks for a galaxy to fully collapse, so she has a little time. Some others might try to escape like her, but you can't evacuate an entire galaxy—there's not enough ships for one thing—especially once the collapse begins and planets start to swirl out of orbit and cause all sorts of calamities and destruction."

Gates agreed. "That's going to happen pretty quickly, stars getting drawn in toward the center and planetary systems pulled apart."

"That'sss a sssobering ssscenario!"

"One thing in our favor," Gates added. "By coming out openly she's branded herself a criminal. She's pretty much cut herself off from Agency and Council resources now, except for her small cabal of followers."

Jeanne nodded. "I suppose that does give us a little breathing room, puts us somewhat out of her reach. Though her new time deadline certainly adds some urgency." Their food arrived. Jeanne accepted hers absent-mindedly, began eating mechanically. She stopped and looked at her plate. "Chicken enchiladas!"

"I requesssted a ssspecial order. It wasss the leassst I could do after your dangerousss misssion."

Jeanne munched appreciatively, gave a thumbs up. "Good! I guess I'm not so over chicken as I thought—even the vat-grown synth variety. What's that you're eating?"

Roingroing held up a carafe-like container with reddish liquid inside. "It isss a ssslurry of protozoa and fungusss from my world. We absssorb our nourisssshment asss juicssse, by osssmosssisss through our ssskin." He inserted a pseudopod into the carafe opening and the liquid began to slowly drain.

"Protozoa and fungus?" Jeanne put her fork down, suddenly not so hungry.

Gates chewed on some sort of crunchy bone-looking treat. That didn't stop him from speaking through the comm in his head. "So, this secret base of Leonore's. Any idea how to find it?"

"Well, she's got her army of toadies following her around, they're not the easiest things to hide. And she had to have supplies delivered, people coming and going. She may think she kept everything under the radar, but it would be hard to conceal something like that."

"Except how would we find out?" Gates objected. "We're still technically fugitives. We don't have access to any official intelligence sources."

"No, we don't. No *official* intelligence sources." A small LED bulb clicked on in Jeanne's head. "But there are other sources, other eyes—lots of little eyes that see lots of things."

Roingroing swiveled toward her. "Who are thessse little eyesss you ssspeak of?"

The LED bulb brightened a few watts. "A mostly unnoticed group who move around the city at will, who already have a large network of information sharing, and who see most everything going on everywhere. Our little flitty-flyer pilot friends, the forest fairies!"

She dug into her enchiladas again, this time with gusto.

* * * *

The screen image cleared on a small face. "Jeanne! Oh-ho! So you did make it. I wondered."

"Hi Trix. I owe you a fare."

"Darn right you do. Thought you'd fallen off the planet. Or a hotel balcony. What happened to audio only?"

"I'm using a consulate terminal. Not secured, so it doesn't really matter."

"I get it. So is this a social call?"

"Let's just say a lot's happened. I could use your help again—and as many of your fellow pilots as you can muster."

"Now that's interesting. Some kind of big-time mission?"

"I'll let you in on it when I see you. If you're willing."

"Well, I'm never one to leave a friend in the lurch. But y'know, we pilots expect to get paid for our services."

"We'll work that out. Believe me, this will be to the benefit of us all."

"Hmm. As long as I don't have to fly you up the side of

any hotels. How soon do you need us?"

"Yesterday. Last week. Let's just meet up, I'll fill you in and then you can coordinate with your buddies."

"I suppose that's the only way I'll collect on that fare you owe me, isn't it? All right. Where?"

"Where you dropped us off the first time. Uh, try to keep this on the down-low as much as possible."

"Mystery and intrigue. I'm hooked already. Be there in twenty." She logged off.

True to her word, Trix's flyer fluttered down to land in the consulate parking loop right on time. Gates trotted out to meet her as she climbed out.

It took him only moments to hack in and direct-connect with her cyber-neural comm, now that he already had the hang of it. "Hello, Trix. Jeanne's in the consulate's meditation dome. Follow me."

"Hey! So you do speak!"

"Only by comms. I don't have the vocal apparatus for actual physical speech."

"Well, I often suspected dogs were more than just humans' pets. In fact, sometimes I think it's the other way 'round, they're your pets. Hard to tell which is in charge."

"You may have something there." He pushed open the gate to the back.

"Say, this's a really nice garden the Spraang have here." Trix breathed in rich fragrances of flowers and vegetation. "I only ever saw it before from the air. Except for the red foliage, reminds a little of my ol' forest home, a long time ago when I was a kid, way back before 'civilization' came." She got a nostalgic look.

They entered the meditation dome where Jeanne and Roingroing waited.

"Glad you made it, Trix. I see you've already adapted to

Gates talking."

"Oh, it wasn't any big adjustment. Do you know how many different species I deal with on an everyday basis?" She plopped onto a cushion opposite Jeanne, took in her surroundings. "Nice little hut here. So what's this big secret mission you need me for? I already figured out you're some kind of government spy or something. Maybe I shouldn't say that out loud. But you wouldn't be working out of this consulate if you weren't."

"The term is 'agent.' We don't like the word 'spy.' I'm actually an ambassador for the Council of Goodwill. But unofficially I'm an agent in the Council's classified Astral Security Division. Gates is my partner."

"Didn't know they had an Astral Security Division. But that explains a few things."

"This meditation dome is a secure place to talk. Trix, I'm going to read you in on something really big, something that will determine the fate of the entire galaxy. Of the whole universe in fact."

"Whoa! Wasn't expecting that. I'm listening."

Jeanne drew a breath and launched into a recounting of all that had happened. Gates showed her the videos of Leonore's test galaxies collapsing. They ended with the latest ultimatums from Leonore, the governments' disarrayed response, and their feeling that Leonore had holed up right here in the city of Lusteer.

Trix sat quietly a long while—a rare thing for her.

Jeanne broke the silence. "Well? Thoughts?"

Trix stirred uneasily. "What *can* I think? That's a *lot* to take in! But I know the Spraang, and they're not prone to practical jokes or hoaxes. So I guess I have to take it seriously. But...this isn't the kind of thing my people normally get involved in!"

"You know what's at stake. You know we're all equally in danger. Neutrality won't work here."

"Yeah." She blew out a long breath. "Guess you're right. Okay, you wouldn't have asked me here if you didn't have a plan. What is it you want me and the other flyer pilots to do? We're not warriors. And we don't have all those high-tech gadgets like you or the government types have."

"No, nothing like that. Just information gathering. You flitty-flyer pilots see more and know more about what's going on around this city than anyone else, right? We just need you to get organized, start looking for anything that could lead us to Leonore's private base, whether it's spotting her toadies, or unusual movements of supplies, equipment, construction materials to one location, that sort of thing. Maybe some of you already saw something like that over the last few months."

"Oh sure. Ever try getting a bunch of my people focused on one thing? Lots of luck!"

"Come on, Trix, I believe in you. Where's that can-do spirit?"

"Well...it's not like I can just tell them this outrageous story and expect everyone to believe it and jump enthusiastically on board."

"No, we actually don't want them to know the whole story. There's too much chance of information leaks that way and Leonore finding out what we're up to. I'm thinking instead that you just put out the word for all flyer pilots to be on the lookout for certain telltale signs, maybe in order to help out some important cause. I'll leave it up to you to decide what will best motivate them."

"Yeah, we forest folk can be a little picky about what causes we get behind. But maybe I can sell it as a search for a really detestable sociopathic criminal mastermind and her fiendish secret lair."

"That's actually not even stretching the truth. Might be stretching the language a bit over-dramatically. But whatever gets the job done."

"I'll have to put the word out on all the flyer comm networks and social platforms and chat channels, get everybody worked up and raring to go—"

"Um, any way you can you keep the comm chatter to a minimum? Don't want Leonore's cohorts—or the governments—listening in."

Trix gave a thin smile. "Don't worry. We'll use one of our native forest languages. There's a couple of dialects we've kept to ourselves and never shared with anyone else, so there's no translation for them."

"Great. Sounds like you've got it covered. I wasn't wrong about you!"

"I'll find a way to make it work. I'd better, anyway." She stood, a little less jauntily than before. "I should get started."

"Thanks Trix. We really need this. Everything's riding on you. No pressure."

"Oh, no pressure she says! This from a crazy person who jumps onto mile-high hotel balconies!"

"Mile-and-a-half."

"Making my point!"

* * * *

After she'd left Jeanne turned to the others. "Any ideas of what to do in the meantime? I have my own thoughts, but I'm open to suggestions from you two."

Roingroing let out a hiss of pent-up gasses. "Ssseemsss to me we have to ssshare our evidencssse with sssomebody. Now that Leonore isss expossssed, ssshould we perhapsss contact your Councsssil?"

Gates answered, "We don't know who within the Council

is part of Leonore's cabal. She could have secret spies anywhere. We'd be taking a big chance."

Jeanne agreed. "Besides which, remember that Leonore put out her rogue-agent label on us. Once you're branded like that it's a hard uphill slog to get back in the Council's good graces, even now after Leonore has been totally discredited. Bureaucratic red tape and suspicion are tough to overcome."

"We could ask the Gu'gundreans to back up our story," Gates said.

"Mmm, we'll probably want to do that before this is all over. In fact, I'd like to meet with them again anyway, find out if they know any more details about Leonore's plan than just the brief flashes I got from them before. Which means risking leaving the diplomatic protection of the consulate and going back into the hotel."

"That should be a lot easier now that Leonore is in hiding."

"Maybe. But it still doesn't help us with the Council or the Agency right *now*. We need something else, something a little more immediate."

No one offered anything. Finally Roingroing spoke up. "You sssaid you have your own idea?"

"Well, this goes back to that half-formed thought I started to have when we were joking about revealing ourselves to the whole galaxy."

Gates sat up. "You're not seriously thinking of doing that?"

"No—at least not yet—considering the total wide-scale screaming panic it would doubtless cause. But Roingroing, you've been listening in on the conversation between the various planetary governments, right? Can you use your consulate comm to patch us in to that conversation?"

"Yesss. But isss that wissse?"

"It's risky. And I won't do it if either of you disagrees. But I'm thinking we come out to the government officials on those classified channels, give them the real story, show them our evidence, the recordings of intercepted conversations—and reveal who we are, too, our Agency credentials and inside information on Leonore. We need to give them better information than just what Leonore has told them, so they can make better decisions and maybe steer away from foolish—and possibly fatal—actions."

Gates said, "That assumes those government officials are thinking rationally."

"Yeah, a big assumption. But if we can influence them even a little, we might actually start things moving in a constructive direction that will stop her lunatic plan."

"I'm not ssso sssure that followsss in their cassse. But it ssseemsss it'sss all we've got. And it'sss better than sssitting on our pssseudopodsss."

"So we're in agreement?"

Gates looked reluctant. "I'll go along, but I don't like it. Even just the logistics of trying to talk to all those governments is daunting. How Leonore expects to get them to agree on anything is beyond me. She really must be nuts!"

* * * *

The logistics were indeed daunting. Just within Lusteer's confederation of seven thousand stars, many more small planetary governments existed and thrived. For expediency and convenience Lusteer oversaw and administered them all—not as some authoritarian power since that had long been discarded as unworkable (Leonore's anachronistic views notwithstanding) but more as a political focal hub or central clearing house.

The same organizational format repeated with every other sector of the galaxy. And the comm network among the different capitols and consulates had long adapted to deal with that sort of thing, with representatives for major conference calls and meetings rotated on a random basis, and AI identifying and grouping those with similar views—it had special direct access to the representatives' cyber-neural implants—and filtering and directing comm traffic and sorting priority communications from routine messages, and so forth.

So what sounded impossible at first glance became in reality merely a frenzied and hectic headache to deal with.

Roingroing set Jeanne and Gates up in his private office with a direct feed from the consulate's communication center, where trans-space monitoring went on continuously (paid for with taxpayer dollars so officials weren't much concerned about costs). Most of it involved standard consulate business. But Roingroing had a secure channel open through confidential consulate sources listening in on higher-level restricted inter-government traffic, behind-the-scenes negotiations and discussions.

The large wall screen carried something over a thousand images of individuals from many species speaking back and forth. Each one represented just the transient tip of a much larger faction of similar diplomats and representatives in their particular galactic sector. The total numbers for each sector showed in illuminated readouts beneath each image, indicating how many planets that individual represented, along with constantly updating and flickering stats for their group that revealed how many other of their sector's representatives agreed with this individual at this moment, how many disagreed, how many abstained, how many had alternative thoughts, how many thought this one was full of BS, etc.

Occasionally two or three would get rotated out—a literal

rotation of the image—and replaced by another as the AI moderator determined the most efficient use and emphasis of time and ideas.

Right now the entire conversation centered around Leonore's latest ultimatum and threats, as evident in the transcribed summary scrolling at the bottom of the screen in Galactic Trade Standard—a conversation that had plainly been going on for quite some time.

Jeanne skimmed through the summary. "Okay, Roingroing, time to patch me in. Is there a way to get everyone's attention?"

"There isss a crisssisss alert sssignal, usssed only in exssstreme sssituationsss."

"I think this qualifies. Hit it."

Roingroing touched a sequence of Braille keys on his desk, then swiped a pseudopod vigorously across all of them at once. The images on the screen all jerked in surprise—some in pain—and those with ears covered them as if at a really loud sound.

"Who did that?" Someone demanded.

"I did." Jeanne saw them all zeroing in on her image on their own screens. "I see that things are going no place fast here. I believe I can change that."

One of the dozen or so human participants, a studious-looking and somewhat gaunt red-headed woman leaned forward. The AI enhanced her image and voice. "Who exactly are you? No one should *ever* use that alert signal except in the most severe galactic emergencies, and certainly not anyone unauthorized! Your comm link is coming from the Spraang consulate in Lusteer, but with no identifying stats or credentials on you."

"Let me transmit them." She nodded to Gates, who had already tied into the comm system. He uploaded their

Council of Goodwill bona fides, Jeanne's ambassadorial rank and title.

He hesitated. "Are you sure this next part is a good idea?"

"Everything."

"Okay, it's your funeral. No wait—mine, too, if this goes south." He added their Agency classified credentials, with qubit-encrypted verification code.

Another of the humans, a pompous balding fellow, called out, "Civil Protection and Astral Security Division? Never heard of it."

"Check the qubit security signature and embedded 3-D stamp."

Another voice from somewhere chimed in, "This is above the security clearance of most everyone here! You're breaking the law just by telling us this!"

"I'm aware," Jeanne conceded. "However, I think you'll all agree this situation calls for exceptional measures. And revealing myself, and the secret organization I work for, is the only way to ensure you'll take what I have to tell you seriously."

A diplomat of an arboreal species Jeanne didn't recognize tried to speak up from its perch on a leafy tree branch, but a third human took over instead, a fastidious and prim androgynous sort—provoking a fit of resentful bouncing and vulgar gestures from the arboreal representative. Apparently the AI had prioritized humans as most likely to relate easily to Jeanne and lead to swift understanding under this crisis alert interruption. "What can *you* add to the 'situation' that we don't already know?"

"A lot. I know Leonore personally. I've worked with her in the Council, as colleagues—though we've recently parted ways in terms of ideologies. In fact I just had a couple of run-ins with her face-to-face. I've seen the weapon she's developed close-up. I know her better than any of you, what motivates her. And I'm pretty sure I know where she is right now."

That last part got their attention. Several straightened in interest.

"Where?" a plurality of them chorused together. The stats under their images flickered and spun rapidly as the numbers of others agreeing shot up by many hundreds of thousands. Clearly this was the question of the day.

"Given the evidence I have, I have good reason to believe she's right here in Lusteer."

A murmur ran through the gathered members. In the momentary commotion the AI rotated several images out and replaced them with new ones.

One of those new arrivals, a yellow-furred and perfectly-groomed humanoid, stood on her feet and yelled, "And what exactly makes you think you know better than all of us, with our many intelligence sources?"

Jeanne waited for things to calm down. "Leonore knows how to manipulate your intelligence sources to her benefit. She's hidden herself well from you, hasn't she? What you do know of her and her plans is only what she herself has told you."

"Possibly so. But do you really think you have inside information *we* don't?"

"I do. Not only that, I have intelligence sources of my own, a network of operatives who are even now scouring Lusteer to pinpoint the location of her hidden base of operations. If anyone can find her, they will."

The new speaker's fur puffed up. "Well I don't think we need to listen to your kind of egotistical rantings—" The AI started to rotate her out. "Hey wait! I'm not done—"

Jeanne didn't lament her departure.

Meanwhile the others had begun engaging in small-group private conferences. Then those exchanged notes with other groups, forming bigger groups or cliques, yet with a sort of overall conspiratorial undercurrent to the whole thing—all while ignoring everything and everyone else. Jeanne felt rudely left out of the conversation.

Finally that pompous balding human cleared his throat self-importantly. "Uh, ambassador, is it? Yes, ambassador, thank you for bringing this to our attention. Rest assured we take this information very seriously. If you do pinpoint Leonore's, uh, hidden base of operations, you'll notify us immediately of course. And now we must deliberate amongst ourselves. Just know that however we act it will be for the greater good." He smiled tightly.

Then the images winked out.

"Hey!" Jeanne said. "They cut me off! Can they do that?"

"It ssseemsss they jussst did."

"Of all the...why do I feel they just gave us a not-so-subtle brush-off?"

"Are you not sssatisssfied at their ressssponsssse?"

"Not even a little. I recognize a run-around."

"Oncssse again your referencesss essscape me, but I will not presss the isssue."

"Gates, did you at least manage to upload our digital evidence to their in-boxes?"

"Yes."

"Then we've done our part as best we can—or as best they'll let us. Let's forget them and focus on what we're going to do next. While we're waiting for Trix to come through, maybe now is a good time for me to pay that little visit to the Gu'gundreans—assuming I can get into the hotel. Wish I still had the shadow cloak."

"We'll sssee that you get insssside. We can sssmuggle you

in usssing a diplomatic pouch."

"A pouch? You're joking. It had better be a pretty big one!"

"Our pouchesss are conssstructed of exssspandable membranesss."

"Of course they are. How are you going to carry me?"

"The sssame way we did from the ssship, with a sssquad of trusssted internsss. We'll desssignate it an officsssial consssulate visssit, a continuancsssse of our Ssspraang hossspitality."

"Okay then. I guess I'm about to find out what it's like to be a baby kangaroo."

* * * *

With the pink diplomatic "pouch" membranes squeezing her on each side like two trampolines, and the Spraang bouncing briskly along, Jeanne felt herself carried very kangaroo-like from the consulate limo into the hotel. Shortly she recognized the unmistakably strong whiff of Gu'gundrean goo, heard the echo of a challenge as someone demanded they justify their presence, followed by Roingroing's muffled response, then the Spraang bounces again as they delivered her the last short way to poolside.

The pouch unzipped at one end. Jeanne did a quick check of her goo suit's seal around her neck, then stuck her hooded head out. Just before slipping into the liquid she caught sight of Roingroing's dutiful guards still standing post around the pool room. Good to know they were on the job protecting the Gu'gundreans—and that there were reliable, dedicated people like that in the universe.

And other reliable people, too. Good people, like the Spraang. And Gates. And Trix and her people. And the Gu'gundreans, too.

She'd needed that reminder. It reinforced her conviction

that Leonore had it wrong, that the galaxy and all its inhabitants—all its diverse races of beings—were worth saving, despite their many flaws and differences and disagreements. That they deserved to live their lives the way they wanted as long as they didn't harm others, deserved to make their own mistakes, deserved to "live and let live."

Wasn't that her sworn oath as Astra Woman, to ensure those ideals, freedoms and opportunities for everyone?

Reasonably reassured, she let herself slide into the translucent green goo, felt the warm womb-like gel surround and support her, felt the now-familiar electric tingles, then the welcoming energies of the Gu'gundreans.

This time matching those energies seemed much easier—and matching minds. Though she still couldn't communicate with words, somehow she seemed to sense what these gentle goo beings intended in a more intimate fashion, as if she were translating their waves of energy into meaning in her own mind, meaning that almost but not quite took on the form of language.

The first thing she sensed was homesickness. The Gu'gundreans were ready to return to their homeworld.

"I understand," she said mentally, pushing the thought outward with the energy flows. "I'd like to help. But I bring grave news, news that affects the very existence of all our worlds, yours as well as mine."

That seemed to produce the appropriate reaction. She proceeded to fill them in on recent events, the highlights anyway, as well as she could, projecting thoughts and pictures and feelings and hoping they'd get at least the gist.

Apparently they did. They became quite agitated at her description of Leonore's weapon and her plan to destroy the galaxy if the governments didn't capitulate to her demands.

After a few moments the largest of them addressed

her. The communication came through more as impressions than words, which her mind sort of automatically converted to familiar constructs in her head, almost like hearing dialogue through her personal comm. "Small limited creature" (that's not exactly what he-she-it-they conveyed, but it's how she interpreted their view of her) "we thank you for this improvement of our knowledge. We wonder what can be done?"

"I'm working on that. I'm trying to locate Leonore, but I don't trust the governments to handle her or the situation right. I'm afraid I'm the only one who knows her and her plans well enough to stop her without getting us all sucked into non-existence. And admittedly what I know is sketchy. What's worse, during the last confrontation I had with her in person, right here in this pool, she showed me she has superior technology—an upgraded sens-suit with greater speed and power than my own. I don't know that I can defeat her in another confrontation if it comes to anything physical. And with her fanatical and fixated beliefs that may very well happen. That's why I've come to you. I'm hoping you can supply me with additional information on what you learned before, anything about what she's doing, possible weaknesses or limitations."

She realized that was a lot, and that her words wouldn't translate exactly, but she hoped enough would get across to matter.

The Gu'gundreans went into hurried conference. Finally the first one turned back to her. "You have given us much of great weight to ponder. We know little of Leonore or her intentions beyond what you do. However, we may be able to help you another way. We perceive that your energy control is more developed than hers, or perhaps hers has become distorted and deformed. While your human grasp of energy capabilities is inherently limited, we believe we can teach you to take your development to the next level."

Jeanne thought she got that pretty well right. She congratulated herself on getting so much better at translating their energy surges. "The next level?"

"From our experience with both you and Leonore, we gather that you understand personal energy manipulation in terms of levels or concentrations you call chakras. That is your name for them, which we consider more a metaphor or organizing scheme. We simply know them as energy forms. To us they are just a natural part of existence, of all the energy forms swirling continually around and through us. To you they are something you must learn to recognize and develop. You humans have identified seven such chakras within your bodies, and five outside or above. There is another, a higher level still, or perhaps something all-encompassing."

Did she get that right? "There is? That's incredible!"

"This higher level is...how shall I put it?...a more whole-istic tapping into cosmic energy. If it helps your scheme or metaphor, you might call it the cosmic chakra. Mastering its use, if you can do so, will give you a more complete understanding and control of all energy forms. In this way, it may allow you to prevail over Leonore."

"Wonderful! Let's get started! Teach me."

"It is not so easy. None of us here has the advanced skill to impart this ability to you. It requires immersion in the streams of energy and consciousness available only in the most suitable environment, and taught only by the most adept of our race. You will have to travel to our homeworld of Gu'gundrea."

Jeanne gave a start. "I will? Oh my."

Chapter 7

"Gu'gundrea does not look particularly inviting," Gates commented as the alien world grew in their forward view screen.

"It isss a world mossstly of goo oceansss," Roingroing offered. "Jussst a few rocky and lifelesss islandsss ssstick up. To outsssidersss it appearsss absssolutely desssolate, which isss why it took ssso long to disssscover it hasss inhabitantsss."

To Jeanne, stuffed once more into one of the courier craft's half-spherical cushions, the greenish goo-world didn't seem all that bad. Almost homey in a way.

Huh, funny thought for her to have. She must have picked that impression up from the Gu'gundreans, some sort of sympathetic harmony or resonance with their minds.

She shook off the eerie feeling. "So how do we land without being stopped by the Council's on-site emissaries?"

"The firssst-contact outpossst hasss ssset up a portable magnetic-lift generator for sssmall vessselsss. I can desssscend on it part-way, then sssswerve off to the ssside in ssstandard atmosssspheric flight before they realize what'sss up. A confidential sssource hasss furnissshed me with a chart from the exsssploration and mapping sssurvey, and hasss asssured me there'sss a sssmall issland in easssy reach with a cave sssufficsssiently large to concsssseal thisss courier ssship."

"Won't they just detect us with instrument scans?"

Gates answered that, as Roingroing had to concentrate on final approach maneuvers. "The islands are mostly electrically conductive metallic ore, just as the oceans are a conductive alkaline medium. According to published scientific reports this entire planet is like that. Which means electronic instruments have very limited effect anywhere here. So inside the cave we should be pretty much invisible to probing sensors."

"Pretty much?"

"This is a scientific and diplomatic station, they don't have anything like military-grade security systems."

"Let's hope."

Roingroing had put the ship into the magnetic descent corridor without responding to queries from the ground, which produced anxious demands to immediately comply or abort the landing. Roingroing ignored those protests and dropped the little craft a bit faster than normal to within a few kilometers of ground, then veered them sharply away toward the encircling gooey green seas.

Skimming the viscous and seemingly endless wavetops Roingroing's concern mounted. "I mussst report that instrument disssruptionsss are worssse than anticsssipated. They sssupply no help finding our dessstination."

"So we're lost?"

"I can only trusssst I've sssstarted usss on the right courssse from the sssscientific ssstation'sss isssolated isssland."

The featureless green ocean seemed to go on boundlessly. But shortly a small black dot appeared on the horizon, and grew into a tiny speck of rocky outcrop standing in lone defiance of the ever-present goo. Roingroing slowed and circled the outcrop, finally locating an overhang with a dark gap under it.

He slowed further and eased them toward the gap, carefully estimating clearances by eye (or whatever the Spraang used), then edged forward until they were fully inside the cavity. He rotated his craft to face daylight and settled onto the cave floor.

"Excellent piloting, Roingroing." Jeanne untangled her limbs stiffly from the too-small Spraang cushion and opened the side door. A tsunami of warm, humid, and horrendously-stinky air invaded the cabin. She winced in involuntary reflex. If she thought the vomit-like stench from the hotel swimming pool had been bad, this outdid that by several magnitudes. Off the scale! At least once she put on her goo suit most of that would get filtered out. Which made her antsy to get started.

She examined the cave interior and opening. "Nothing lives in here?"

"There isss no life anyplacssse on the surfacssse, even microorganisssmsss. Only in the oceansss."

Jeanne walked up to the cave mouth, looked out over the uniform and unchanging seas. If she didn't already know intelligent lifeforms lived in there she'd have no clue. "You know, I think our instruments being useless here is part of why no one discovered the Gu'gundreans before now. We've gotten so used to relying on gadgets that almost no one ever does manual work on the ground anymore—or in the goo."

"A sssensssible sssupposssition."

"But that raises the question: didn't any earlier survey ships wonder why there's oxygen in the atmosphere here?"

"Csssertainly. Photosssynthetic microorganisssmsss that convert sssunlight and basssic chemicalsss into oxygen and sssugarsss. That'sss what makesss the goo green."

"Which ought to suggest a food chain with possibly more sophisticated or 'higher' lifeforms, just as with any ecology. Hmph. If they'd just stuck their heads down into...well, maybe I can't blame them for not wanting to do that. Anyway, the sooner we get started the sooner we can get out of here before someone from the scientific station does come knocking." She collected her goo suit from the courier ship and struggled into it.

As a last preparation she opened a carry compartment in the ship and retrieved a soccer-ball-sized translucent sphere the same color and gel-like consistency as the goo, except it had a molecularly-manipulated tough outer skin and felt resilient in her hand like a water balloon. The Gu'gundreans on Lusteer had described it as a sort of memory globule, a molecular-energy recording of the conversations they'd had together. But more than that, it supposedly contained all the thoughts, feelings and energy exchanges they had shared— the total experience. They said she should present this to whoever she first met here, so they'd learn all that had already transpired, as well as prove her friendly intentions and save a lot of time.

She especially liked the "prove her friendly intentions" part, seeing as how she was about to become an unknown interloper into these beings' private world. Trespassing was universally frowned upon by all species, even by lower animals. And these guys had some powerful electrical energies at their disposal.

She picked her way down over raw, jagged rock to the shoreline. Apparently this world had never invented sandy beaches. The island just dropped off steeply and the ocean took over.

A large and somewhat smooth boulder seemed her best bet for ease of ingress. She worked carefully toward it, sat on top and pivoted her legs around to face the lapping waves and swells. So far no sign of gummy-worms—or electric eels. Looking down she could see no bottom to those pastel depths like she could with the swimming pool.

Well, no time like the present. She scooted forward and

dangled her feet into the slimy liquid, already feeling those electric tingles. No way to ease in a bit at a time, she held the memory globule against her abdomen, pushed off and let herself plunge fully in.

* * * *

The electric tingles exploded around her in a cacophony of raw currents, an unexpected and overwhelming shock to her system. The energy flows in the hotel swimming pool had been intense, but these assailed her in incredibly more powerful and complex torrents and patterns, a whole civilization's communications traffic whizzing every which way, like the difference between a whispered conversation with one person and an entire auditorium full of everyone yelling at once.

Her suit compensated with increased electrical resistance and O_2 output, and things receded to something more tolerable. She took in her surroundings. Still no gummy-worm creatures. She did see a few small jelly-fish-like lifeforms undulating by, and what looked like schools of tiny fish though lacking tails or fins or heads. Must be part of this planet's food chain.

Without warning a large shadow rose up out of the depths, rushed toward her with swift purpose. Right before reaching her a more familiar translucent eel-like shape swooped in just as abruptly from the side, intercepted the shadowy creature with a thump and forced it off into the murky distance. She sensed subsonic pulsings as if from a silent struggle, then quiet.

Shortly the eel-like shape returned, swam slowly around her, evidently looking her over. Jeanne had the unsettling feeling she'd just barely escaped experiencing this planet's food chain first hand. She summoned what she'd learned from her previous energy communications with the

Gu'gundreans, said, "Uh, thank you."

The creature halted as if surprised, drifted in front of her. Then it extruded a small bump from itself, almost like the beginnings of a Spraang pseudopod, pointed in the direction of the memory globule in her hands. That must have been what had attracted it to her—or what had prompted it to save her from that shadowy thing.

She held the globule out, offering it as instructed. The Gu'gundrean touched it with its bump-extension and it immediately disintegrated into its constituent molecules, dissipating into the fluid around it.

"Hey!" Jeanne sent out the thought. "You just destroyed my best means of communicating with your people, my letter of introduction!"

The creature pushed its bump into the space where the globule had been, and electrical blue sparks crackled and sizzled, spreading outward in little tracks throughout the liquid medium. The Gu'gundrean paused a moment as if absorbing some of those energies.

Then it addressed her in much the manner established back on Lusteer: "No, I did not destroy it, I liberated it. It is now part of our world, available to all sentient beings here."

Jeanne didn't question their ability to communicate in something approaching words. "I see. Then you know why I've come."

"Yes, and your urgency. Follow me." It turned and began swimming away.

She tried to comply. "Uh, I'm afraid I have little ability to move in your environment."

The Gu'gundrean returned to her, seeming to consider the problem. It narrowed the last several inches of its body into a tail-like shape. "I perceive you have grasping members. Hold onto me."

Jeanne started to do so, then hesitated. She was in their world now, not hers, and this might be a bit more complicated than she first thought. "I should tell you that my species cannot tolerate pressures at great depths. We need to stay near the surface." She tried to express the approximate depth with pictures, allowing a liberal margin of error to account for the greater density of gel versus water.

"I understand. I will respect this constraint." It offered its tail again. Jeanne took it and the Gu'gundrean set off once more, whipping her disconcertingly back and forth from its swimming motions.

She found herself whisked along speedily, so fast that resistance from the viscous gel almost tore her loose. She had to activate her sens-suit under her goo-suit to increase her grip strength.

The journey lasted longer than she liked. But eventually they arrived at what appeared to be a large conclave of similar goo-beings of all sizes and amorphous shapes, thousands or more stretching off into the hazy distance. Even so, it didn't seem so crowded as her encounters on Lusteer. But then they had a whole planet here, not just the confined space of a swimming pool.

Once again she sensed the constant exchange of energies coursing among these beings, an intimate connection or sharing, all centered around family and friendships and organized society, the typical activities of a vast and ancient civilization. Though they had no way to construct technology or infrastructure as humans understand it, Jeanne did see more of those molecularly-hardened skins like the memory globule had, only on a much larger scale, from huge globes to enormous enclosed areas like pens or maybe farms, and sheets of delicate-looking lace-like material in artful designs, with occasional connecting strands and lattices, some glowing with strings of lights— more bioluminescence like some marine life had on Earth. But all of it obviously intelligent and deliberate, and beautiful in its own exotic way.

Her guide, moving more slowly now, threaded among the undersea city's buildings and thoroughfares (her brain couldn't resist converting this totally alien setting into familiar human terms, inappropriate as that was). Eventually they came to a stop at a large open ring like a city center or amphitheater. Several dozen goo-beings milled there, and more arrived by the minute. Jeanne got a feeling of great reverence and respect enveloping the entire place.

Her guide withdrew its tail and turned toward her. "This is a communal gathering center, a place of discussion and decision for this part of our world. In your terms you would probably call it a seat of government, though that translation is imperfect. It is a place where all are heard, and all ideas compared against our highest principles. Here your request will be considered and judged." Then it spun and sped away, leaving her suspended alone in the middle of the amphitheater.

Another government confab. Great. Just what she needed.

More goo-beings crowded in, lining the ring around the edge until she felt hemmed in on all sides as well as above and below. The electrical energies intermingling and pervading the place, at first random and casual, slowly took on the patterns she'd experienced with the Gu'gundreans back on Lusteer and that had been captured in the memory globule—it reminded her very much of a review and debate. Gradually the cluttered conversations began to align, forming into something more coordinated, more synchronous, almost harmonious. Almost like...music?

She felt, in a very inadequate analogy, as though an orchestra of many instruments and sections playing many independent parts, and trying many themes and variations and melodies and counter-melodies, finally weaved those parts together until they resounded in one crescendoing chord.

And from that chord came the unified thought: "We agree."

Then the arena's attendees spontaneously swirled and dispersed outward into the surrounding ocean, leaving only a handful remaining.

Huh, Jeanne thought. Did she just witness government by music—or its electronic equivalent, anyway? Now there was a novel concept! But why not? Music was expression, yes, but also mathematical proportions of intervals and waveforms, rhythm and timing, harmony and dissonance and resolution—what better way to run a civilization?

In the relative quiet Jeanne faced a few lingering Gu'gundreans serenely observing her from the sidelines. "You must be the adepts I'm supposed to learn from."

"We are," came the united reply.

"I'm ready. When do we start?"

"We already have. We have been studying your overall energy patterns and how well you integrate them with everything around you."

"Oh? How am I doing?"

"Not good—woefully deficient by our standards. We perceive you are incapable of ascending to the highest levels, at least without first working step by step through all the lower levels you have not yet mastered."

"Well that's why I'm here, right? To learn from you."

"Regrettably, it is simply not possible at this stage of your development."

"Now just a second, there must be a way! You know what's riding on this!"

"We do." They went into a private huddle. Jeanne sensed some disagreement. At last they turned to her again. "We admit you have the potential to activate your higher levels with appropriate guidance. Unfortunately that undertaking would require much concentrated effort and time—time we don't have given the imminent threat to the galaxy. However, there may be a compromise solution."

"That's better. Let's hear it."

"We can imbue you with a subtle if tenuous connection to the higher energy level—the cosmic chakra, you call it—just a taste so to speak. But one that with only a little training you might be able to trigger in a time of intense crisis and that would grant you at least partial access to this greater energy realm. It could give you a temporary boost at a moment when you most need it. No guarantees, though."

"I'll take it. What do I do?"

"Nothing. Just open yourself to us and let us do the rest."

"I can do that." Jeanne inhaled deeply from her suit's recycled O_2 and relaxed into herself, letting her cares and concerns go, calling on her prior meditation and energy work, then reaching outward to draw in the energies and perceptions around her.

She didn't really feel much happening during her "training" session. The adepts performed some sort of energy manipulation on her, so they said, then had her look inward to her energy centers, find the core of herself, and extend this to everything surrounding her. They wanted her to sense a connection to some all-permeating cosmic energy both existing independently of her and extending from within her at the same time.

She wasn't sure how successfully she accomplished that, even after meditating on it a good while—quite a while it appeared, though she lost sense of time along the way. At one point she did kind of flash on something like a new, very brief and very nebulous energy channel opening somewhere around or above her. But she couldn't pin it down or be certain.

They told her to call upon this new awareness in moment of great need, and that she would know how when the time came. That sounded way too vague for her liking. But they terminated the discussion at that point, dismissed her and disappeared into the gooey deep.

* * * *

Not feeling terribly encouraged or very different, Jeanne let another guide—or maybe the same one—conduct her out of the arena, back through the "city" and on into open ocean, and finally to the rocky island where they'd found her. Just before parting ways she heard the advice, "Do not tarry. We do not normally keep predators in check here." Then the guide, too, vanished.

Jeanne heeded the warning and heaved herself out of the soupy liquid as hastily as the extra strength of her sens-suit permitted, then scrabbled up the rocky shore to where Gates stood in the cave mouth, tail wagging. She pulled off her goo-suit's hood, gagging at the sudden unfiltered influx of stench, and began peeling out of the rest. "Time to leave. Fetch me that hermetically-sealed bag from the ship, would you? This goo-suit needs to stay in there until we get it seriously power washed."

"Did you get what you needed?" Gates asked. "You were gone a long time."

"That's the question. We'll find out, I guess. Did you guys have any trouble?"

"A hover vehicle flew by once, checking out the island by sight. But we stayed well hidden."

"Good. Does Roingroing have an exit plan off this planet?"

"He says that without instruments they can't track our flight. He intends to gain as much altitude as the courier craft can, then enter the magnetic lift corridor high up where we won't be easily spotted by eye. They shouldn't detect us until we're already inside the lift beam and well on our way out of the atmosphere."

"That sounds a little iffy."

"Again, scientific and diplomatic station—no great security or surveillance capabilities. They only keep the lift beam on because it holds a few scientific packages aloft to physically monitor weather and ocean changes."

"If you say so. Let's get going."

They clambered into the courier ship where Roingroing already sat in the pilot seat setting up his departure calculations. Jeanne sealed the door and wedged herself into a passenger couch. "Ready when you are."

Roingroing touched his controls, the ship lifted off the cave floor and glided out into the open, oriented itself in the direction they had originally come from, then streaked toward the sky.

They must have climbed several kilometers before leveling off at the courier craft's maximum altitude for in-atmosphere flight. After a while the scientific installation came into view ahead, set on the planet's largest island but still only a speck in the all-encompassing ocean. From this height they couldn't make out any details—but that also meant they made an even tinier speck to anyone on the ground.

Roingroing flew them straight into the magnetic

monopole lift beam and powered up his ship's repulsive magnetic generator, which swept them swiftly the remaining way above the atmosphere like a leaf in an updraft.

About the time ground control noticed the small fluctuation in their beam strength and put out a demand to "identify yourself!" the courier craft had cleared all nearby mass and Roingroing could punch in his pre-programmed sub-quantum FTL leap for home.

* * * *

Return to Lusteer went off without complication. The little vessel entered one of the city's many descent corridors, joining with other typical traffic of the day: countless vehicles coming and going, carrying people (of all species) and cargo. Roingroing's diplomatic pre-paid toll pass let them skirt past customs and entry-fee stations without needing to stop.

Meanwhile the city's inhabitants, and the whole planet of Lystrom Two, went about their normal affairs, their relationships, their business dealings, their politics, their work, their recreations, their loves and lusts, their deceptions and quarrels, unaware of the grim danger threatening their existence—a scenario played out in duplicate in all the other innumerable cities and planets throughout the galaxy.

Roingroing steered them adroitly through the gleaming-tower obstacle course of Lusteer's capitol and finally into the Spraang consulate garage, where the dome's petals closed around them. Back safely on firm ground, they retreated immediately to the consulate's meditation dome.

Roingroing had broken Spraang etiquette and installed a comm terminal there for convenience, a decorum violation justified only by the extreme necessity of their situation. Jeanne immediately put in a call to Trix.

"What is it?" This time Trix looked harried. "Oh, Jeanne. Wasn't expecting you, but glad you called. Been trying to get in touch with you."

"I had to take a little side trip off-planet. Did you manage to locate our target?"

"It's been a challenge herding these fiercely independent compatriots of mine, I won't lie. But...is this comm secure?"

"I wouldn't count on it."

"Then best we meet in person. Same place?"

"Sure."

"Be there soon." She logged off.

They didn't have to wait long. Gates went out to meet Trix and escorted her into the meditation dome where she collapsed onto the cushions, looking beat.

"You must be putting in quite a bit of overtime," Jeanne remarked. "Gates, order her some refreshment and something to eat."

"Thanks," she responded. "But just some forest-moss tea, if you don't mind. With that one spice you humans have— what's it called? Cinnamon."

Jeanne said. "What did you find out?"

Trix pushed to her elbows. "You were right. We tracked the arrival of those toadies you were talking about, and their movements all lead to one location."

"That's big news! Where?"

"It's some sort of underground fortified compound near the edge of the original city's old quarter, maybe a military installation left over from the first human occupation here, but abandoned long ago. You guys did a lot of secretive stuff back then, some of it not so honorable. But I won't get into old resentments."

"Yeah, sorry about that."

"Well, things are pretty good now, thanks to all of us

working together through cooperative galactic covenants. Or most of us. Anyway, shipments in and out of this underground compound suggest Leonore has secretly been refurbishing part of it for some time."

"That's got to be her base of operations! Great work, Trix. Can you show us on a map?"

"Better. I've got it in digital aerial view, topographical view, street view, whatever you want." She held out a tiny plastic rectangle smaller than a fingernail.

"Is that an actual physical data drive? I haven't seen one of those in ages!"

"I didn't want to trust anything that could be hacked wirelessly."

"Smart. Gates, this is your wheelhouse." She took the drive and stuck it to a universal data port on his collar. He opened the 3-D map and projected the image into the air. It showed the city with its cluster of capitol towers and diplomatic center, the surrounding commercial districts, sports stadiums, residential areas, space port for larger vessels, the old quarter off to one side, and not far from there a mostly abandoned and overgrown section with a big red X marking one complex of buildings. "You certainly made that plain enough."

"Didn't want you to miss it. Play the time-lapse flyer-cam video we patched together and you'll see those toad guys trucking supplies in over the last few weeks."

They did so. Jeanne whistled. "That pretty well clinches it. Okay, so we know where she is. Now we have to figure out how to get to her—before her deadline runs out."

"Won't be easy. Like I said, she's holed up in an underground part of that base. And those toadies make up a small army guarding every entrance and exit."

Roingroing broke in, "Ssshould we not leave thisss now

to the governmentsss? We're sssuposssed to inform them asss sssoon asss we've dissscovered Lenore'sss posssition."

"True," Jeanne mused. "They did say that. And they are certainly better equipped to handle this than we are. All right, fine. I'll put aside my misgivings and hope they actually follow through from here. Roingroing, go ahead and set us up with another conference call. Uh, can we do that now after they cut us off last time?"

"I can ussse a more officsssial consssulate channel inssstead of my persssonal one. That ssshould at leassst essstablisssh an initsssial conectsssion."

"Let's do it. Trix, go get some rest. You probably want to remain anonymous with these government reps, anyway."

"You bet! Anonymous is my favorite thing to be when it comes to government."

* * * *

As before, the comm screen in Roingroing's private office came alive with myriad little images of diplomats engaged in energetic debate, several caught in the process of rotating in or out and displaying various degrees of indignation at the AI moderator. But before Jeanne could say anything the screen went blank.

Then it returned with only one large image in place of all the others: that pompous balding human that had dismissed her so curtly the first time around.

He narrowed his eyes. "You again. This better be good."

Jeanne regarded the enormous bloated face filling nearly the entire screen, every pore and imperfection visible in magnified detail. He did not look healthy this close up. "I'm here to speak to the whole assembly," she said. "Put me on, please."

"Well, you see, due to the sensitive nature of our discussions and the need for secrecy, and to best streamline communications and ensure effective action, I have been chosen by unanimous consent to stand in for all."

Spoken like a true politician. She doubted that "unanimous consent" part, too. "I see. That's highly unusual, and contrary to any standard protocol as I know it. You'll appreciate my skepticism."

"These are unusual times. We must adapt, make a few concessions if we are to accomplish our mutual ends."

"So? I'd still like to address the conference directly."

"Out of the question. Moreover, you are not actually part of our conference, so technically you have no right to address anyone here. I'm showing you a courtesy just by acknowledging you at all. Now, do you have something to say, or are you just wasting my time?"

Jeanne drew a breath, calmed herself. "Very well. You asked that I contact you once I'd found Leonore's location."

He leaned forward with curiosity. "And have you?"

"Yes."

"Well why didn't you say so? Let's have it!"

"Understand I'm doing this out of civic duty, and I expect you'll use the information appropriately and follow due legislative procedure."

"Yes, yes! That goes without saying."

"Does it? It had better. Transmitting now to all the representatives' in-boxes." She gestured to Gates, who uploaded the map data.

It arrived via compressed-dimension trans-space messaging, and the man looked it over on his screen. He furrowed his brow, mumbling something about "under the old military base" and "hardened against conventional weapons."

Finally he looked up. "We'll have to confirm this, of course. But you may have actually proved useful after all."

"So what are you going—" Jeanne started to say.

But he severed the connection.

"Hey! He cut me off again! And I didn't even find out what they plan to do. That guy's really starting to get on my nerves."

Gates tried to reestablish the link. "Yup, they completely locked us out."

Jeanne brooded. "I thought our government was supposed to be open and transparent. That's a laugh."

Gates said, "Let me try to hack a work-around. They may have blocked our direct comm, but maybe I can re-acquire the confidential back-channel chatter, at least listen in and find out what they're up to."

"That would help. We can't just sit here and do nothing. Leonore's deadline is fast approaching. How much time do we have left?"

"Two days, counting today."

"Two days till doomsday! Yeah, I'm not leaving that up to government inefficiency—or arrogant clods like that guy. Gates, do your hacking thing. I need to think."

She left the consulate building and withdrew alone to the meditation dome, sank into modified lotus position, then took several deep breaths to de-stress and clear her mind. She needed clarity right now, some degree of perspective. The dome's peaceful, reddish bio-lit ambience helped.

She tried to connect with her higher energy centers, maybe even that new cosmic energy she thought she'd glimpsed ephemerally back on Gu'gundrea. Nothing came easily, though—too much anxiety. And as for that higher cosmic energy...not even a glimmer.

After awhile the door slid aside and Roingroing rolled in softly. He closed the door and sat opposite her in silence. Jeanne opened one eye half-way, then went back to her meditations. But she could still feel him there.

"All right. What?" she said finally.

"Sssorry to disssturb you. I jussst wanted to know your intentssionsss."

She exhaled in exasperation. "I don't know. We're completely cut off from what the governments are doing, we're still on the outs with the good part of the Council and my Agency. And we seem to be the only ones who know what's really going on. But I don't see what we can do about any of it. And we have only today and tomorrow left! What about you, do you have any ideas?"

"I mussst confesss I'm ssstymied."

"Then we're in a heck of a pickle, aren't we? Don't ask what that means, I'm not in the mood."

Neither spoke for some time. Finally Jeanne got up. "This is getting us nowhere. Let's go see if Gates had any success hacking back into the restricted inter-government comm traffic. Never hurts to be better informed about the major players."

They returned to Roingroing's office, found Gates pacing nervously, listening to the comm channels on low volume.

"I take it you got something," Jeanne said.

He stopped pacing. "Oh, I got something all right. But you're not going to like it. It's bad, *really* bad!"

"Bad. Okay, what is it?"

"It may not have been such a good idea to tell them Leonore is here in Lusteer, dug in under a fortified military bunker. They've been in secret closed session, debating and taking votes, and...well maybe you should hear for yourself."

"Can't you just summarize?"

Gates shook himself. "All right, I'll try. It started as a proposal pushed by one small but dominant faction among the planets, presented as the only doable option. It gained momentum quickly, and now appears about to be adopted as an official resolution!"

"*What* is about to be adopted?"

Gates shuddered. "They think the only way to save the galaxy, the only way to get at Leonore before she can trigger her weapon...is to completely annihilate the entire city of Lusteer!"

"*What?*" Jeanne and Roingroing exclaimed together.

"They see it as an 'acceptable trade-off.' For the greater good."

"Greater good? Seriously? That's the same phrase Leonore used, the same excuse she gave for what she's doing!" Jeanne felt staggered. She leaned against Roingroing's desk. "Can we break into their session? Use that emergency alert signal like we did before?"

"They've blocked us even from that. I'm afraid all we can do is listen."

"Gates, turn up the sound."

He did so. But the vote had just happened. The resolution had passed, and the order went out for an automated nuclear strike: best delivery time to target, tonight, eleven p.m. local time.

Roingroing let out an anguished squeal and deflated to about half his normal size.

"How is this possible? Those kind of weapons haven't been used in centuries. They're banned!

Gates gave a helpless shrug. "Evidently they still have some in stockpile. They'll have to pull one out, replenish its depleted nuclear material, fly it in special."

"I don't believe this," Jeanne sputtered. "It's insane! 'Greater good.' The governments want to sacrifice a whole city for the greater good. Leonore is willing to sacrifice an entire galaxy for the greater good! How far can you take that logic? Greater good is a seriously messed-up philosophy!"

"It doesss ssseem to be usssed to jussstify lotsss of horrendousss thingsss," Roingroing conceded.

"Well, we can't let them get away with it. We have to stop them—but now we have to stop both Leonore *and* the governments." She shook her head. "It seems our job just got a *whole* lot harder."

Chapter 8

"It gets worse," Gates said.

Jeanne threw up her hands. "How can it get any worse!?"

"They're planning to blame it all on you."

"*Me?*"

"It's that balding guy and his power bloc. They're already drafting a press release pointing to your rogue agent status, claiming you're a crazed revolutionary who smuggled in a banned nuclear device to carry out a terrorist attack, and that only their quick and heroic response stopped you from destroying more than just one city."

"That's...."

"CYA on a galactic scale."

"I'd say!"

Roingroing put out a pseudopod to pat her comfortingly on the shoulder.

Jeanne filed this new and incredibly unfair injustice under "grievances to deal with later." She composed herself as best she could, said, "Okay, but that doesn't change anything. We're not going to let them wipe out an entire city just to take out one person. No! We need to get into that underground bunker, locate Leonore and stop her personally, one-on-one. Then find a way to notify the governments and get them to call off their strike. All before eleven p.m. tonight."

Gates gave a snort. "Oh, so nothing too difficult then! Aside from fighting through an army of toadies, how are we supposed to contact the governments when they've completely blocked our communications with them?"

"The only thing we know of that can hijack their communications is that emergency interrupt signal. We've got to figure how to get that back. That'll be your job, Gates, your number-one priority. Once we do that and we've got their attention, we can *show* them we've neutralized Leonore and taken her into custody."

"Uh huh. Sounds simple. Which is why I know it's not."

"Brainstorm with me here. I'm working backward from the end scenario."

"Right. Okay, well we know Leonore's already got a direct line in to the government reps, that's how she's making her threats and ultimatums. We can piggyback on that once we're into her secret lair—and assuming I can hack into that emergency interrupt signal again. Problem is actually muscling our way into that secret lair past its many guards and defenses. I know Astra Woman is good, but even she has limits."

"Don't I know it! I've already had one confrontation with those toadie mercenaries, and it's going to take every skill and techno-advantage I have to get through a whole platoon of them. Where's an invisibility cloak when you really need one?"

"You've got me!" Gates said helpfully.

"My gallant champion. But your most important job—*the* most important job—is to get us that comm channel, and to bypass any security systems we encounter on the way in. We can't risk you physically fighting if we can avoid it."

Roingroing had been listening from the sidelines. Now he spoke up. "Perhapsss I can be of sssome sssservicssse?"

They looked at him. "You?" Jeanne said. "No offense, but your species isn't exactly built for battling armed military types."

"It'sss true we are a peacssseful ssspeciesss. But we did not sssurvive thisss long without natural defensssesss. We have learned to ussse our intelligencssse to exssstend thossse defensssesss when necesssary."

"Okay, I'm intrigued. What kind of natural defenses?"

"When ssstartled we producsssse and dissscharge noxsssiousss gasssesss that ssscare off or disssable predatorsss. We have trained oursssselvesss to do ssso at will, and to adjusssst the composssition of thossse gasssesss to sssuit the sssituatsssion. Thisss can become an effective offensssse asss well asss defensssse."

"Oh? I wasn't aware. But I don't want to put you in any situation where you're in peril."

"Are we not in peril already? The mossst exssstreme peril? Alongsssside the entire cssssity—and galaxsssy?"

"Uh...fair point. And I'll admit I could use some back-up. A knock-out gas sounds like just the what we need. All right, if you think you can handle it, you're in."

"So how do we do this?" Gates pressed. "We don't even have blueprints for that underground rabbit den. We'll be going in blind."

"That's where you come in. When we get close enough and you can connect to even part of their security system, you'll be able to gain inside info that you can feed to me and Roingroing. You'll be guiding us one step at a time."

"That's not exactly a solid plan!"

"Unfortunately we don't have time to finagle every little detail, we have to do this tonight. So yeah, we're going to have to wing it to some extent."

"Great. The fate of the galaxy hangs on us winging it!"

"Pretty much. Now here's how I see it going down...."

* * * *

Their strategy session went on longer than intended, well

into the night, while the deadline crept closer. Finally Jeanne called a halt and rang up Trix again.

"Trix, we need your taxi services one last time."

The little forest fairy yawned and stretched, then snapped to wakefulness. "What do you mean one 'last' time?"

"Nevermind. Just get here soon as you can."

"Already here. Slept in my flyer. I'm right outside on the consulate landing loop."

"You're a peach! Hope you can accommodate the three of us as passengers."

"Well, the Spraang don't add much weight, so as long as one of you sits in someone else's lap it shouldn't be a problem."

"As it happens, Gates likes my lap. We'll be right out."

As they hurried from the consulate building and across the parking lot Jeanne glanced up at the stars overhead, the shiny towers of the capitol all around, the glittering city lights, the other air traffic still buzzing with purpose even this late. It struck her suddenly that this might be the last time she ever got to witness those sights.

She got into the flyer with grim determination, helped Gates jump onto her lap, while Roingroing bounced lightly into the other passenger seat. Trix closed the canopy, powered her flyer's wings up to speed and they lifted into the air.

Trix broke the glum silence. "Should I guess where we're going?"

"You probably can. Leonore's underground compound."

"So? But just to reconnoiter, right? You're not going to do anything foolish."

"The less you know, the better for you. You can drop us off far enough away that you won't be spotted."

Trix looked apprehensive, but flew them onward without

further comment.

Finally the city's main outskirts thinned out below and merged into the old quarter. Adjacent to that the long-abandoned military complex lay in complete darkness, overgrown with moss and vines, to all appearances uninhabited and lifeless even in the midst of teeming signs of civilization all around.

Trix angled in steeply and came to rest just outside one end of the base, with the low silhouette of a large concrete structure dead ahead in the distance, a dark and mute testimony to humanity's violent past—and to its potential for violence still slumbering not far beneath the surface.

"That's where Leonore's underground bunker is," Trix said as she opened her flyer's canopy, "right beneath that central building. Seems to have been some sort of bomb-proof shelter or HQ. There's only one entrance, you can just make it out from here."

They could: a darker mouth-like gap in the middle of the structure. Between it and them lay a scattering of newer-looking shipping containers of various sizes stacked in a seeming random pattern, but that Jeanne suspected had been deliberately placed to impede anyone's direct approach by ground.

"What I wouldn't give for some high-tech detection gear and a little air support. Or just a good pair of night-vision binoculars." She got out. "Thanks for the lift, Trix. You can head home now."

Trix's expression grew worried. "You're going in, aren't you? This isn't just a reconnaissance mission!"

Jeanne showed her an earnest smile. "You've been a real help—and friend—through all this. I value everything you've done. But now we have to do the rest on our own." She transformed into her sleek, youthful Astra Woman persona, her sens-suit contracting to hug her body and provide its many enhancements. Then she motioned to Gates and Roingroing and the three of them set off at a jog toward the base HQ building.

Trix watched them go. Finally she put her flyer into a climb and lifted away.

* * * *

The first hundred meters toward the bunker went without incident. While the shipping containers were meant to hinder, they also provided cover. Though the entire base remained totally dark, Jeanne's sens-suit detected several heat signatures and movement up ahead close to the building itself, relayed directly into her brain through the cyber-neural circuitry in her head.

Abruptly a blinding sizzle erupted in the night and one of the shipping crates next to them exploded in a blaze of sparks.

"Down!" Jeanne yelled, ducking behind another stack of containers. "That zapper blast was set to kill!"

Roingroing quivered, but recovered quickly this time. "It ssseemsss they've ssspotted usss."

"That may only have been a warning shot. I doubt they know who we are yet."

"A warning shot set to kill?" Gates asked incredulously.

"The toadies have their own idea of morals." Jeanne reached out with her sens-suit, tried to determine what the mercenary sentries were doing. They all seemed grouped around the building entrance in a defensive perimeter, about twenty of them.

She addressed her companions again. "All right, we knew this might happen. So I'll draw their fire to the right, Roingroing you see if you can sneak around upwind of them on the left to release your knock-out gas. Gates, hang back until you see a safe opening and can get close enough to connect with their security system. But don't take any unnecessary chances! That goes for all of us. We've got no help coming if one of us gets in trouble. Everybody ready?" She checked the toadies for any change. "I go first. Roingroing, wait until they see me before you move."

She got into a sprinter's starting position behind the crates, then took off at a run to the right. She hadn't gone ten meters when another zapper plasma blast hit close by her—too close. She put on a burst of speed and made it to another stack of containers, paused there and looked back to see Gates watching anxiously. But Roingroing had already gone.

She took off once more, zig-zagging among the crates in a hopefully unpredictable pattern while dodging the continuing plasma bursts, always working closer to the bunker. Only her heightened Astra Woman athleticism and sens-suit's extra speed gave her the edge and confidence to pull off such a reckless feat. So far she hadn't used her speeded-up time sense, because for now she just had to keep the toadies focused on her so Roingroing could do his part.

After covering about half the distance to the bunker she paused again and tried their private comms. "Gates, Roingroing, are we still in comm range?"

"I'm here," Gates replied.

"Ssso am I. In posssition and ssstarting to releassse gasss."

This much closer now, Jeanne could more clearly see the toadies guarding the entrance. Suddenly the ones upwind started coughing and waving their hands in front of their faces in revulsion, then the others began doing the same.

But they weren't collapsing in unconscious heaps like they should. It looked like they were just reacting to a really disgusting smell.

"Roingroing, what's going on? Why isn't it working?"

"My gasss mixsssture may not be precissse yet. It'sss a processs of guesssing and tesssting."

"And you couldn't have told us that earlier? Try another mixture."

"I need sssome time to regenerate the necesssary chemicalsss."

"Well regenerate fast. A stinky smell isn't going to get us inside that building. And it's drawing attention your way. Those toadies are looking for the source of the smell. You'd better get out of there—now."

Jeanne saw a pseudopod shoot out from a hiding place not far from the building, then a beach-ball shape zoomed out behind it at remarkable speed. The shape rebounded off another stack of containers, contracting and elongating as it flew and shooting out more pseudopods like rubber bands to propel it along. The toadies reacted with zapper fire but Roingroing's surprise erratic flight confounded their aim. He disappeared down field near Gates' position before they could get a bead on him.

Jeanne chuckled. More of those Spraang natural defenses, she supposed.

But now a bevy of toadie reinforcements poured out of the bunker's door to join their mates.

"Guys," Jeanne said, "we've got trouble."

The new group added to the first totaled about twice as many as before. The reinforcing troops didn't stay bunched up near the door, either, but spread out in a seek-and-find pattern. It wouldn't be long before they discovered her, and then Gates and Roingroing.

"Hunker down, boys, I'm going to try something." She keyed the mental code to kick in her speeded-up time sense. The more those toadies spread out the easier they made it to dash unhindered among them with her enhanced reaction time. She didn't expect to get by the squad still amassed at the door, but right now she had something else in mind.

As the first of the searcher group drew near she darted out, side-swiped his burly toad-like body and spun him around with her momentum, grabbing his zapper pistol away from him with her souped-up reflexes in the process. She left him in mid-topple and launched toward the next, did much the same to him. Then as other toad-arms started swinging guns at her in subjective slow motion she raced away toward the place she'd left Gates.

She skidded into the shelter of containers as a zapper blast sizzled the pavement where she'd just been. Gates greeted her with joy.

She slowed her time sense enough to have a normal conversation. "Roingroing, where are you?"

"Here." A pseudopod waved from behind the next stack of crates over.

"How's that knock-out gas coming?"

"Nexsssst batch needsss ssseveral more minutesss to finisssh."

"We don't have several more minutes. Here, take this." She slid one of the two confiscated zapper pistols over to him. "Can you shoot?"

The pseudopod touched it tentatively. "I am not violent!"

"You don't have to be. But those toadies are converging on us fast, and we need to defend ourselves if we want to stay alive. Set your zapper to 'snooze'—that's the lowest non-lethal setting."

Jeanne's time-slowing trick had bought them a few moments, but she hadn't counted on this glitch in their plans. If it had just been her she could have easily gotten around these guys, but with the responsibility of two companions she didn't have that luxury.

"We need to hold them off until your knock-out gas can do its job. Get ready!" Keeping low she took aim around the crates at the first approaching toadie, waited until she couldn't miss. "Now, Roingroing! Zappers on snooze, fire!" She squeezed the trigger.

The big lug went down like a shoddy high-rise in a major earthquake. She took out the one behind him just as quickly, then saw another fall—Roingroing had joined in. Between the two of them they forced the toadies to reconsider their rush-'em-in-the-open strategy and scatter to cover.

In the temporary lull Jeanne said, "This won't last. They have us outnumbered and outgunned. We need that gas!"

"Almossst finissshed."

"Make it quick. Can you direct its dispersal?"

"To sssome exsssstent. I can ssspew it in a ssspecific directsssion, but then air currentsss take over."

"Good thing you're still upwind. Will it harm us?"

"Thisss mixsssture ssshould not affect humansss or dogsss."

"Another 'should,' huh? We've had a lot of those lately. Well, we're about to find out if you're right. They're getting ready to rush us again." Her sens-suit detected renewed activity among the toadie troops, then a coordinated forward movement. "Here they come."

They advanced in two waves, one running upright as before and the second wave squatting on all fours and *leaping* like actual toads. Aside from reversion to type, it lowered their profile and made them harder to hit.

Too many! Jeanne zapped three or four but they'd be overrun in seconds. "Roingroing!" she called out.

Abruptly a sickly-sweet vapor like a room-fragrance aerosol filled the air, and the lead attackers clutched their throats in distress, gasped and staggered, then keeled over. Jeanne got in a couple more shots, but the remaining toadies had sudden second thoughts and retreated hastily.

"Great work, Roingroing! That should hold them a little while. How long before you can whip up another batch of that gas?"

"It will go much fassster now that I've essstablissshed the correct mixsssture. But isss it not sssensssible for usss to retreat alssso, sssince we have the chancssse?"

"We can't. I *have* to get into that building. Everything depends on it. And for this to work Gates needs to gain security access, so we have to get him in there, too."

The toadies who'd remained at the bunker door now hustled up to assist their comrades. Some of them started taking pot shots, but from a safe distance and shielded by containers. Jeanne returned fire randomly just to keep them honest.

"We ssseem to be ssstuck in a ssstalemate," Roingroing observed.

"Yeah, and the clock's ticking. If this goes on too long we'll never make it in time to stop the nuclear attack. Either of you got any brilliant ideas?"

They did not.

The toadies began making occasional rushing attempts now, but Roingroing's gas and Jeanne's marksmanship repelled them each time. Jeanne thought of going into overdrive again and trying to bypass the lot of them, though with so many her chances weren't terrific, especially once she made it to the bunker door and had to slow down to break in. Even then she'd have left Gates behind, so that wouldn't do.

Guess this plan had more flaws than she'd anticipated. So much for winging it.

She imagined them stuck in this standoff indefinitely, or at least until more toadies arrived to break the stalemate in Leonore's favor—and then the unthinkable happening as she and Gates and everyone else in the city vaporized in a blinding flash of heat and gamma radiation.

Just when her desperation had reached its boil-over point and she'd concluded she had no choice but to rush in by herself, yet knowing that without Gates or Roingroing she'd almost certainly fail, another voice broke in on their private comm channel: "Anybody order taxi service?"

Jeanne looked up. Behind them, just above the skyline and faintly illuminated by city lights, a whole swarm of bees bore down on them. No, flitty-flyers! Dozens, a small armada, descending on the base with a loud collective thrumming sound.

"Trix! Is that you?"

"I told you I never leave a friend in the lurch. Hope we're not too late."

The first few flyers swooped in overhead, shining lights down and dropping soccer-ball-sized translucent spheres onto the toadies below where they burst like water balloons. Jeanne thought the spheres looked a lot like that memory globule she'd gotten from the Gu'gundreans.

The drenched toadies yelled in pain, swatting at their exposed skin and running in futile circles.

"What in the world?" Jeanne exclaimed.

Trix answered, "Yeah, I got a tip you'd been working with the Gu'gundreans. So I paid them a visit over at the hotel—one of my third cousins knows a guard at the pool. They were only too happy to supply us with these goo-bombs. Thought we ought to give Leonore's troops a little corrosive alkaline bath."

"Ooh! That's got to hurt."

More flyers joined the party, diving and flitting around in a kind of semi-ordered chaos. But the uninjured toadies fired up at the flyers, too. Jeanne saw one get hit and go down, then another. She hoped the pilots were okay.

About then a raucous commotion of yelling voices came from the end of the base closest to the old quarter, getting nearer, and Jeanne saw a mob of the most unlikely assortment of species hurrying across the field and into the fray, brandishing whatever armaments they'd managed to scrounge up, mostly clubs and other hand-to-hand weapons. She spied a lumbering Hougranian galloping surprisingly fast and swinging a pair of heavy sledge-hammer-type mallets, its small fur-ball sharp-toothed male mate riding atop its head behind its eighteen eyestalks, cheering her on.

A tall Zebra-striped Loper strode swiftly by like a stately land schooner, a K'ttn on its back. The K'ttn gave Jeanne a wink of recognition and a cat thumbs-up, then they plunged into the melee with a cat-howl battle cry. Jeanne shook her head in amazement.

Other misfit denizens from the old quarter or who-knows-where charged into the brawl with equal enthusiasm. Shouts and body blows clashed with the sizzle of zapper fire. But the overwhelming number of volunteer militia and the effectiveness of the goo bombs quickly turned the tide in their favor.

As fighting died down Jeanne looked over the battle scene. The toadies that hadn't run away lay writhing on the ground, completely out of action, or were held down by citizen enforcers.

Trix spoke on their personal comms again. "Okay, your path's clear all the way to the front door. I suggest you avoid the wet spots, though."

Jeanne grinned in wonder. "Trix, I don't know how you

pulled this together, but you're a lifesaver—maybe a city saver in this case! Oh, and thank all your other friends here for me, too, especially your flyer buddies. Gates, Roingroing, let's go."

She set out for the bunker, Gates and Roingroing on her heels. A familiar ratty-looking flyer fluttered in close above and trailed them to the door, hovered until Gates had hacked the first security level and the massive armored doors hinged open.

"This is as far as I go," Trix said finally, "Good luck." She banked her craft away and into the night sky.

* * * *

Inside the door a long hallway yawned before them, wide and airy and bare, and low-lit by what appeared to be a line of small amber emergency lights near the ceiling.

Jeanne's sens-suit showed no signs of presence—living or mechanical—in the area immediately ahead, though several ominous-looking wall emplacements poked out along the length of hallway. "Security defenses?" she asked, waving her captured zapper pistol in their direction.

"Disabled," Gates assured her. "Along with their sensors. I have full security access for this first part of the building."

"Where's the underground entrance?"

"Up ahead, around a corner. There's a transport elevator and a stairwell."

"Lead the way. Better shut the door behind us so no curious locals wander in and get hurt. And stay on the lookout for more guards. They can't all have gone outside."

They started forward warily, Roingroing bouncing as discreetly as he could. The hallway had no side doors; evidently it had been designed to funnel all visitors in or out and nothing else, under the watchful threat of those defenses. Though disabled, Jeanne kept a close eye on them just in case.

They made it to the elevator and stairwell without difficulty. Gates called a halt. "This is tricky," he said. "Security here is even tighter than at the front door. I need a minute."

"Don't take too long. We're on a clock."

"This system is more primitive than I'm used to, which I expected since this is a very old base. But it has something like internal self-preservation algorithms and lots of redundancies. Military software, I'm guessing. There's an AI running everything, but it's very primitive, too. Ooh, I'm not sure it likes me. I think it's gotten grumpy from sitting around this abandoned base for the last couple hundred years."

"Don't bother with that, just get us downstairs."

"You want to find out where Leonore's set up camp, don't you? Then I have to make nice with the resident AI. There— I've got security control for the stairwell now. We can start heading down."

They did so, remaining vigilant for guards, Jeanne stretching the sensing abilities of her sens-suit to the limit. The stairwell, wide but plain and austere gray-painted concrete, befitted a military installation. Still they met no resistance, only the echo of their footsteps and Roingroing's somewhat fretful bounces.

"Maybe all the toadies really did go outside?" Jeanne remarked as they descended past a block-letter wall stencil that said sub-level four.

"More likely the rest are marshaled around one spot to protect Leonore. Okay, I'm starting to get the hang of this system. All life services—lighting, heat, water, electrical power, ventilation—are limited to sub-level nine."

"Sub-level nine it is."

While they encountered only standard high-impact security doors on the first eight sub levels, sub-level nine had much thicker and tougher armor. This must be that "hardened against conventional weapons" classification. Gates had some trouble hacking the locking and alarm mechanisms there, but by getting more chummy with the AI he persuaded it to relent and let them in.

As the heavy portal swung aside Jeanne sensed movement just beyond it. Then a barrage of zapper blasts painted the opening with heat and bright sparks. Jeanne held everybody back, waited until their antagonists got tired of firing pointlessly, ramped up her accelerated time sense to its max and zoomed inside.

Only two guards crouched in what appeared to be a small room like a security checkpoint. She quickly disarmed both, then stunned them with their own zappers. As they crumpled unconscious she beckoned her companions in. They seemed to move in excruciating slow motion until she returned her time sense to normal.

Gates looked around at the room: bare save for a guard desk with reinforced Plexi-steel shield. "Good thing you've got me along. This place is loaded with hidden defenses—electronic, chemical, sonic, kinetic. If you had come in here without me...well, let me have a crack at that next inner door."

Jeanne moved aside to let him work. Much like an airlock, the security checkpoint had both inner and outer access to control who or what got through. Gates defeated this second mechanism handily and had it open in seconds.

Jeanne checked the hallway beyond: still devoid of opposition, just another long empty corridor. But this one had branching hallways leading off in every direction.

"Any idea which way?" she asked.

"Hold on, I'm searching for recent power usage and systems activation to see which route's had the most traffic. But with only near-field access it's kind of like sniffing out a scent, or picking up a trail of bread crumbs—you only get the next bit in front of you. All right, got it. Three corridors down on the left."

They proceeded cautiously. Once again Jeanne's senssuit showed a clear route. If Leonore had more guards she really was playing them close to the vest.

This secondary corridor branched into even more tertiary corridors, which Gates guided them along, emergency lighting coming on as they went. If not for him and his ability to connect with close-by electronics they could easily have become lost in a vast underground labyrinth. Maybe that was Leonore's tactic: let them meander aimlessly around down here forever—or until the galaxy folded in on itself.

Jeanne began to get restless. They were seriously running low on time. "How much farther?"

"How long is a trail of bread crumbs? Answer: pick up each one and find out."

They kept on doggedly (a literal term for one of them). Finally Gates stopped. "Hold it, I'm getting something different."

"What?"

"A large energy draw up ahead in one confined area. Same for ventilation and water and sewer. Looks like a center of activity."

"That's got to be Leonore's hidey-hole!"

"If so, it's a big one."

"Come on!" She hurried forward alertly. And now she began sensing life forms gathered farther ahead—quite a few, though her readings were spotty, reflected and absorbed by numerous dense walls and bends and turns among the maze of passageways. She slowed as they drew near. "On your guard. We're about to crash a good-sized party."

Only a few paces more and the first party-goers ambushed them from a side corridor—or tried to. Three of them. Jeanne detected them in advance, kicked her time sense up again and overpowered and stunned them before they could do any damage. Same thing happened at the next intersecting corridor and four more toadies took a nap.

Then the passage rounded a bend and opened into a larger chamber where at least a dozen troops stood spread out in military formation, ready and waiting. Jeanne didn't wait, as those many zappers began firing immediately. But "immediately" to them and to Jeanne with her sped-up time sense meant different things—especially since normal perception takes at least two- or three-hundred milliseconds to travel from eye to brain and then out to a muscle in response—so she had already weaved among the lead troops, disarming them as she went, before the first blasts left their guns.

She saw Gates duck down low to avoid those blasts, but she knew she wouldn't be able to get all the toadies in this room before someone got really hurt.

That's when Roingroing surprised her. He went into a kind of overdrive himself, more of his natural defenses she supposed, sprang suddenly forward (was that how his species got their name?—naaah), slammed directly into one of the toadies, instantly rebounded off him and into another using pseudopods as guides, then another, and so on like a pinball bouncing rapidly back-and-forth between bumpers in a crazy pinball game, with a trajectory that ultimately took him across the room.

That wild bumper-car flight disoriented the toadies and gave Jeanne enough time and distraction to finish relieving their opponents of their weapons. Two or three tried to take her on physically, but found themselves promptly zapped, either by her or by Roingroing who had picked up a couple of weapon souvenirs in his whirlwind tour of the room. The rest backed off.

Gates trotted over, snarling menacingly at the toadies along the way. Jeanne edged up to the door leading to the next room, the one these guys seemed to have been defending, and took a quick peek inside. A medium-sized chamber, but no guards in evidence. In fact, not much of anything.

She slowed her time sense again. "Roingroing, hold these guys at bay. If they get froggy, gas 'em."

"I'm sssorry, my gasssing abilitiesss are exhausssted. I need nourisssshment to replenisssh the necesssary chemicalsss before I can producssse more."

"Then just look mean and intimidating. Gates, any automatic defenses in here?"

"I already took them offline."

"Watch my back." She inched forward. This next room seemed truly empty. Part way across she turned to give the all clear to Gates when she caught a slight movement out of the corner of her eye: a wavy ripple in the air.

Recognition flashed in her mind: shadow cloak! Instinctively she ducked just as a flare of light and a sharp shock jolted her to her core and everything went black.

* * * *

She awoke dazedly to the sound of Gates growling and a nearby scuffle. As her vision slowly swam into focus she saw her canine guardian with his jaws clamped in a death grip on the arm of a toadie, the two of them locked in a tug-of-war, the shadow cloak lying on the floor deactivated alongside a zapper pistol.

She did a quick check of her suit's systems. It had protected her from the full brunt of that blast, as had her abortive attempt to duck, but she still felt shaken and woozy.

She crawled the short distance to the zapper pistol, set it to "extra-super-snooze" and shot the toadie, then collapsed back to the floor.

Gates released his hold and hurried to her side. "Are you all right?"

"Give me a minute. Or a week." She felt her rejuvenation nanobots working to repair and restore what they could, but how long that might take—or how successful they'd be—she didn't know.

She eyed the shadow cloak. Not something you could buy at your neighborhood convenience store. Probably the same one she'd lost in her fight with Leonore's private guard on her weapon ship, then. This soldier likely took it as a spoil of war, and thought it fitting to use against her here in a kind of personal revenge. She should have expected that.

On the other hand, once she got her strength back she could make good use of it now. Assuming she got her strength back.

Her suit began to regain some of its functions. She noted that Roingroing still held the entrance to this room, and no one approached from the other direction.

But...one suit readout didn't look right. "Gates what time is it? Local time."

"Ten-forty p.m."

"What? How long was I out?"

"Awhile."

She struggled to a sitting position. "We've got to get moving! You know what happens at eleven p.m. Help me up."

"You're in no condition to do any more fighting."

"With this cloak I hopefully won't have to. But none of us will be in any condition for *anything* if I don't get my butt in gear."

Gates put his head under her arm and helped her to her feet. She swayed unsteadily.

He looked her over. "This isn't good. You've already been in rejuvenation mode too long as it is—I think you know it. And then getting zapped on top of that...."

"I don't really have a choice. Anyway, I'm feeling better now, honest." Had she said that to convince him or herself? She picked up the shadow cloak and zapper pistol, faced the next door in line. "I need to get in there. Can you unlock that?"

"I think so. But you should know, I've got no connection to anything from that point on. There's some kind of next-level advanced cyber-neural blocking I've never encountered before. Whatever's on the other side of that door, it's an electronic blank, a complete void. I have no clue what you'll meet in there."

"That's...a little ominous. But this is where the bread crumbs lead, right? Everything points us to that door. So that's where I need to go." She slipped the shadow cloak over her head, activated it, keeping the alien pistol concealed close in front of her. "Ready. Go ahead, do it."

Gates gave a gruff woof of disapproval but triggered the locking mechanism. The door slid aside to reveal another long narrow corridor with armed toadies spaced along it at intervals. They all turned to point their guns at the open doorway.

In her head Jeanne said, "Gates, stay! Hold your position. As long as you don't approach they shouldn't shoot. These are Leonore's elite private guard, her last bastion of defenders, charged with protecting her person at all costs. They won't leave their posts for any reason."

"Which means Leonore must be—"

"Just down that hall. We're definitely in the right place. All right, you stay here and keep their attention on you while I try to sneak by them in this cloak. Do your growly thing to seem threatening but don't get shot. We just want them focused anywhere but on me."

"Got it." He faced the guards, head down, legs spread, teeth showing, a low growl building in his throat.

Slowly Jeanne slid up to the doorway. Fortunately she'd had plenty of practice with this cloak now to know how to move in it without giving herself away—she hoped. But as long as the guards were looking elsewhere and not expecting a very slight visual distortion sliding along the wall, she thought her odds were pretty good.

She got past the first one by keeping flat and as close to the wall as possible. Gates helped by giving a couple of low barks to keep the fellow's mind on him.

"Good job, Gates," she said in her head.

He didn't answer.

"Gates? Are you there?" Still no response, though he stood just outside the door only a short ways from her. "Roingroing? Can either of you hear me?"

Nothing. So that cyber-neural blocking must be jamming her signals, too, in here. But her sens-suit and shadow cloak still worked. So it must be only the comms and near-field stuff that were affected.

She kept on, got past the next guards. But toward the end of the hallway one seemed to notice something suspicious and turned his attention her way. She froze.

Gates saw it, barked and lunged at the door. One of the toadies reacted by taking a shot at him, and that diverted the rest enough for Jeanne to slip on by, while noting thankfully that Gates had anticipated the shot and sidestepped it without harm.

At the end of the corridor she paused again and peered through an open doorway into another large chamber. This one had the look of a control or command center with a lot of old computer equipment, none of it working. But against the far wall a bank of very active modern screens and comm system had been added, and a high-backed swivel chair on a raised platform.

And in the chair, back to the door, she saw a familiar wavy gray-haired head. Jeanne stepped quietly into the room.

The chair swiveled around and Leonore looked straight at her. "Well, well. Here you are again. Amazing how you keep turning up. By the way, that shadow cloak will do you no good with me. My new and improved sens-suit can see right through it. No pun intended." She grinned smugly while activating her own rejuvenation protocol.

Behind Jeanne the door slammed shut, cutting them off from Gates and Roingroing and the toadies and everything else, leaving them alone together.

Chapter 9

Jeanne shrugged off the cloak.

Leonore stood, now the youthful and super-fit version of herself, her own sens-suit with its enhanced capabilities hugging her body just like Jeanne's. She gazed down from the edge of her raised platform at the zapper pistol Jeanne held. "Oh, sorry to disappoint you, but that pistol won't work in here, either. Suppression field. Drains all those types of energies. Our predecessors who built this place were pretty paranoid about their personal security."

Jeanne checked the weapon. Sure enough, it's charge registered "dead." She shook it to be sure, then let it drop next to her cloak. So much for that idea.

Leonore went on, "I'm truly fascinated by you. You won't give up. You have these grand ideals—false ones, of course. But you must realize you've played your last card and you're out of moves. Kudos on getting past my defenses—I've been following your progress since you first entered this base. But now your energy is depleted, you've been in rejuvenation mode too long, and you're injured. You can't beat me."

"Do I need to? Can't we just have a reasonable conversation?"

"Mmm. Why not? I am a bit bored waiting for the government assembly to respond to my ultimatum. They'd best get a move on, though, deadline's close, only a day away now. So what's on your mind? And don't think you can just use this as a stall tactic to give yourself more time to recharge from that zapper blast, because even that won't do you any good."

"No, no, I realize that." Jeanne did acknowledge her general weakness. Despite running on adrenaline, she could feel the intensely deep strain of everything up to now, of all the fighting, of staying in her rejuvenated Astra Woman form far too long, of using her speeded-up time sense well past its design limits. It had all really begun to catch up with her.

Add to that Leonore's upgraded sens-suit and Jeanne had no delusions of defeating this woman physically. She had to approach this another way, get Leonore to reassess things, maybe question her belief system. It might be a long shot at this point and with so little time left—Leonore's deadline may still be a day off but the nuclear attack would happen a *whole* lot sooner. She couldn't give up now, no matter how epically worn-out she felt.

She said the first thing that came to mind: "You talk about ideals, and mock mine. But don't you see that *your* ideals have consumed you, distorted your view of everything, led you down this dark and destructive path?"

"Oh, must we go through all that again? I thought we'd hashed this out in insufferable detail before. I have no interest in revisiting old territory. If that's all you've got, you've wasted your time."

Jeanne tried another tack. "You're really going through with it then?"

"With what? Imploding the galaxy? Only if the governments don't yield to the inevitable. But I don't make idle threats, because those don't work. So, worst case scenario, and for the greater good of all other galaxies in the universe as a whole, yes. I'm willing to do what's necessary and set an example here."

"They won't, you know. Yield to your demands."

"That remains to be seen. They will if they're smart. Unless you know something I don't?" She eyed Jeanne curiously.

Jeanne caught herself. She'd almost let slip that the governments knew her location and had already made their decision to obliterate this whole city in the next few minutes. That negative information just might provoke Leonore into setting off her weapon early.

Instead she said, "You know what your own Agency is calling your weapon, don't you? The Great Galactic Goodbye Gizmo."

Leonore scowled. "I've heard this nickname through my own sources. It's insulting and demeaning, a childish coping mechanism of people ignorant of any greater purpose."

"Is it? They think your weapon, your whole Plan, is a joke. Oh, they know it's real, they've seen the evidence. But they regard it as self-indulgent and narcissistic—monstrous on one level but intellectually laughable on another." She knew she was pushing some psychological buttons there, but maybe that's what she needed to do.

Leonore waved away the affront. "No matter. In the end history will vindicate me. Is that all you came here to do? Throw cheap insults? I rather expected more."

"I came to talk you out of this one last time, to appeal to that more compassionate Leonore we once looked up to, to get you to see reason."

"Really, Jeanne. This is getting tiresome. So unless you—" Something drew her attention to her monitoring consol. "Huh. It seems your SPOT companion—Gates, I think you call him—is attempting to override this base's AI. Clever, that one. He might even succeed, too. He's already cut off my communications to my guards outside. I'm afraid I can't allow that. I rely on that AI too much—which in hindsight may have been an oversight, but then I never expected anyone like you to show up. Well, I'll just have to stop him myself before he does any further damage. Move aside." She stepped down from her platform and advanced toward Jeanne.

Gates! What was he up to? Jeanne planted her feet and held her ground in front of the door.

Leonore must have lost patience. She went into sped-up reaction time and launched herself forward. Jeanne initiated her own hyper-speed subjective time just as Leonore reached her, throwing them both backward forcefully into the wall. They clashed in a whirlwind of grappling limbs and augmented sens-suit strength, Jeanne doing her best just to hold her opponent off in self defense.

But it quickly became evident that Leonore really did have the advantage, not just because of her faster and stronger sens-suit but because Jeanne could feel her body's energy and overall vigor diminishing by the second. She'd pushed herself too far and now she was about to pay the ultimate price.

Leonore got the upper hand easily and wrapped her arms and legs around Jeanne in a painful scissors squeeze, something Jeanne herself had done many times before with recalcitrant adversaries—though without Leonore's murderous intent. Only Jeanne's own sens-suit kept her from being crushed.

But she couldn't keep it up. She didn't think she could last much longer. She was going to fail—probably die—right here, and let everyone down, everyone in the whole city, maybe in the whole galaxy, all sentient beings, all her friends, and Gates....

No! Something inside her welled up in rebellion— determination, yes, but something else too, almost as if a voice spoke to her from some dormant place in her mind. No, not so much a voice as a sense of knowing, of wisdom imparted from master to student, saying, "Energy is not just in the body. Now is the time to open yourself to that higher place, that all-permeating cosmic energy existing both independently of you and extending from within you at the same time. Reach out, become part of this energy, feel it flow through you. Take charge and direct this flow."

Somehow a part of her actually seemed to know what that meant, and even how to do it. She relaxed and centered herself, opening a connection to that higher energy, a tenuous but definite channel to something altogether new to her experience, something indefinable, something...cosmic.

And it did open, and blossomed, expanding and filling her with a sense of light and warmth and calm—and vitality and strength.

That strength enveloped and infused her entire being, as if she'd become immersed temporarily in a vast pool of universal luminance. Without thinking she broke Leonore's hold and pushed her away. Leonore stumbled back in surprise, then came at her again with redoubled fury. Jeanne deflected the blur of arms and legs, grasped a wrist and twisted it around behind Leonore's back, got hold of the other one and held them there firmly.

Leonore sputtered and tried to squirm loose. "What the devil! How—?"

"I've had a little upgrade of my own."

Leonore struggled fiercely, but to no effect.

Just then a welcome voice came into Jeanne's head. Apparently her comms were back online. "Jeanne!" Gates said. "Are you all right in there?"

"I've got things under control for the moment." She'd added the "for the moment" because she already felt her extra cosmic-energy boost beginning to fade, to her dismay. "Can you get in here?"

The door slid open to show the elite toadie guards all lying inert on the floor. Gates stepped over them. "Me and the base AI are buddies now. Once I got on its good side it wasn't hard to turn the automatic defenses against these jokers and hit them with military grade snoozers. They'll be out for a good long while. What about *her?*" He pointed his nose at Jeanne's prisoner.

"Can you find something to tie her up? Check the toadies, they ought to carry some kind of restraints."

Gates did so, came back with two-inch-wide ShrinkTite™ bands used by law enforcement. Jeanne slapped them around Leonore's wrists and ankles, made sure they sealed completely. They'd been constructed to hold even the strongest known aliens and even most robots, so she felt sure Leonore couldn't break out of them—a good thing because she felt her strength waning fast. And she had to hold on awhile longer because they weren't done here yet, not by a long shot, if the clock in her much-abused sens-suit had it right.

Roingroing came bouncing up the hallway. "The guardsss are all unconsssciousss. What elssse did I misss?" He saw Leonore trussed up on the floor. "I sssee your were sssuccesssful."

"Only partly. We still have to contact the governments and show them that Leonore's been neutralized, get them to call off their strike. Which we have precious little time to do—less than two minutes!" With her mounting fatigue she found it hard to stay focused, and she couldn't afford that. "It may be too late already. How long does it take to turn around a nuclear attack? Gates, you've got to get us that emergency interrupt signal *now!*"

"Oh, didn't I say? That's the first thing I did, with the AI's assistance. The assembly has actually been watching us for some time. They pretty much saw your whole fight with her. Check the monitors."

Jeanne looked over at the bank of screens on the wall. The now-familiar checkerboard of little government images stared at them, several in the process of rotating in or out. "You saw?" she inquired.

One of the images, the studious-looking and gaunt red-headed woman who'd first challenged her during their initial meeting, took center stage and spoke up. "We did."

"Then you know Leonore's safely in custody and no longer a threat. Call off your nuclear strike!"

"Well now, whether or not there ever was such an...uh, extreme contingency plan ordered, which we can neither confirm nor deny, I assure you the alleged warhead has definitely been disarmed and is being redirected harmlessly into an ocean."

"So the city's safe?"

"It is."

"And the galaxy's safe?"

"We're still confirming that, but we have very high confidence. Our tech analysts tell us that someone there working with the base AI has scrubbed Leonore's data systems completely, fried her weapons control, wiped everything—even the automatic remote one on her weapon ship—so the weapon can no longer be triggered. We can dispose of it safely now."

A massive weight lifted off Jeanne's shoulders. Tension drained out of her, along with the last trickle of her energy.

"The AI also sent us Leonore's personal files, which lists the identities of her lieutenants. It looks like she kept all real power for herself and the rest are basically lackeys. So they should be fairly easy to round up." She spread her hands. "It seems we owe you an apology. We dismissed you too lightly—Ambassador Jeanne." Then she leaned forward with concern. "Uh, are you all right? You don't look well."

Jeanne slumped to the floor, relieved, utterly exhausted, and spent beyond all endurance. No, she did not feel well, not well at all. She felt quite the opposite of well.

Just before passing out she heard that same person's voice demanding: "Someone get this woman a medic!"

* * * *

Dream visions fluttered like flitty-flyers through Jeanne's half-formed consciousness, sometimes in the form of Gu'gundrean gummy worms floating around her like watchful guardians, sometimes like Trix ferrying her on some important and secret mission while keeping up a steady stream of social gab, sometimes like Roingroing bouncing along releasing gases and nervous hissing then suddenly breaking into his crazy imitation of a pinball playing bumper cars with shadowy foes. Shadows, shadow cloaks, shadowy spheres of strange matter, oceans of goo, Leonore's smug sneer...they all blended together in a swirl of surreal impressions. And Gates wouldn't stop licking her face.

Vaguely, she heard voices: "...strain was too severe...not much hope...tried everything we can...can only wake her for a short while...."

She labored up from a deep well, managed to choke out hoarsely, "Gates, stop licking my face. I can't hear what they're saying."

Gates did stop, then started in again with zeal. "You're awake! You're alive!"

"Are you sure? Doesn't feel like it. I ache everywhere, my head's spinning, I can't lift my arms." She appeared to be in a hospital bed. Several species of doctors, both organic and robotic, stood around her solemnly, while medical machines beeped and hummed and a holo image of her insides glowed in the air a couple of feet above her. Something about that medical scan didn't look right, though.

Roingroing bounced onto a stool by her head. Gates stopped licking and settled down to lay on her stomach, his tail thumping rhythmically against her legs.

She tried to get her thoughts in order, but found that oddly hard to do. "Just tell me, did I dream it? Or did we pull it off?"

"It'sss real," Roingroing assured her. "We sssucceeded and everyone isss sssafe, thanksss to you."

"Wonderful! Then why do I feel so incredibly bad? Like I'm not all here. Kind of...flimsy."

One of the robo doctors rolled up to the head of her bed. "We've brought you out of coma with stimulants and extraordinary measures. Unfortunately that is the limit of what we can do. All of your body's systems have been severely overtaxed, beyond ability to repair. I'm afraid that, despite the best efforts of modern medical science, your internal organs are shutting down, your cells self-destructing one by one."

"So...I'm dying."

"Yes."

She absorbed this news with a strange detachment. "How long do I have?" But she already knew the answer. She felt it.

"Moments."

She closed her eyes and let the reality sink in. Then she looked around the room at her friends, and at all these other beings. At least there still was a room and beings to fill it. "Roingroing, thanks for all you've done. I'm glad we got the chance to know each other." She smiled tearfully, even as she felt her consciousness begin to slip away, the flimsiness growing ever more pervasive. "And Gates, my faithful canine companion." He stood and looked intently into her eyes. "I'm sorry to leave you now. But...it looks like this is my own Great Galactic Goodbye...."

His goofy and worried face evaporated into darkness as her vision faded. The last things she heard were his howls of grief.

Chapter 10

Jeanne's eyes flickered and she became mindful of a quiet background humming, and gentle warmth surrounding her. Dead? Not dead? Or was this another dream?

Overhead ceiling lights came into focus, and the pale blue walls of an ordinary room. She lay in a shallow bath of sorts, a clear green gel or goo, but without her goo suit. She stiffened, expecting to be burned by alkaline chemicals.

"Relaxsss. You are sssafe."

"Roingroing?" She spotted his pink dodge-ball shape beside her bath. Funny, not only did this gel not burn, it actually felt pleasant and smelled flowery. She tried to sit up.

"No, ssstay immerssssed. It'sss facsssilitating your healing processs."

"I don't understand. I thought I was supposed to be dead."

"Ssso did we. But the Gu'gundreansss, asss you know, have excsssseptional waysss of manipulating molecular chemisssstry. They applied their exsssspertisssse to your cssssellular necrosssisss and producsssed both internal ressstorative therapiesss and thisss sssusssstaining sssupportive emulsssssion."

"You mean...they fixed me?"

"With the asssssisssstancsse of your Councsssil, who sssupplied an updated versssion of your rejuvenatsssssion nanoware that correctsss for many limitationsss of the older versssion. In concsssert with the Gu'gundreansss, who ssshared their natural regeneratsssion abilitiesss to infussse your cellsss with propertiesss analogousss to theirsss, you ssshould be asss good asss new sssoon."

"Wait a minute. Regeneration abilities? You're not talking about...*immortality?*"

"Not exsssactly, no. But it doesss ressstore sssome youthfulnesss, and they asssure me you will live a long and vigorousss life yet. Jussst how long they can't essstimate, but csssertainly longer than ssstandard for your ssspeciesss."

Jeanne took this in. She imagined little Gu'gundrean goo globules coursing through her bloodstream—no that couldn't be right. But she couldn't get the highly unscientific image out of her head. "I do seem to be feeling youngish, almost semi-rejuvenated," she admitted.

"Yesss. There are sssimilar ressultsss, but without the dangerousss ssside effectsss. And on a permanent basssisss."

At that moment the door slid open and Gates bounded in, stretched up over the side of the bath and began licking her face again.

"Gates! Okay, get it out of your system. Yes, I love you too, but that's enough, please." She patted his head with a goo-soaked hand. "Can someone please tell me where I am, and how long I've been here?"

Gates calmed down, fell back into his service canine role. "You're in the infirmary of the Stellar-Hyatt hotel—actually a convalescence suite just off the infirmary. The Gu'gundreans wanted to keep you near their swimming pool so they could monitor your recuperation. You've been out for several weeks."

"*Several weeks?*"

"In an induced state of suspended pseudo-life, or so the Gu'gundreans tell us. I don't think anyone really understands their process but them."

Roingroing added, "Gatesss volunteered asss a tessst sssubject at each ssstep of that processs, before they tried any exsssperimental techniquesss on you—with the end resssult that he hasss all the benefitsss of exssstended life, too."

"Really?"

"Yep! I feel like a young pup again, eager to chase balls and squirrels. Looks like you're stuck with me for a long time to come."

"That's great! But...leave the squirrels alone, please." Jeanne lay back and let all this wash over her, along with the goo gel.

"Meanwhile, much has happened," Gates went on, "if you're ready for an update."

"Absolutely. I'm dying to know how things turned out. Wait—poor choice of words. Not dying, *living*. Fill me in."

"There's been a major shake-up on all fronts. By exposing Leonore and her cabal, we've made the Goodwill Council realize its own internal rot. They've done a deep cleanse of the entire organization and swept out the bad apples. What's more, they recognize your pivotal role in making it all possible, your unswerving devotion to its highest ideals. So—get this—they want you to take over as Senior Councilor and head of the Council."

"What? Now wait a minute! *Me?*"

"And they want you to revamp its entire structure as your first priority."

Now that was highly unexpected. She thought about it. Head honcho of the whole organization and pretty much a blank check: a tempting offer.

But that very temptation alarmed her. How easily had Leonore succumbed to the corruption of unlimited power, regardless of how well-intentioned she had started out? That possibility, that temptation would always exist.

She shook her head. "Uh-uh, no. That would just be repeating past mistakes. *No one* should have that kind of power and control, not me or anyone else."

"But the Council needs someone to lead it."

"Does it? The Council must be revamped, without doubt. But it can be restructured in a more decentralized way. Something more egalitarian, without hierarchies, where all members share in every decision and policy. Same for our Agency. All this internal secrecy and control—it needs to be abolished. It's clearly corrosive. I mean, Gates, just look at you. Didn't you think it weird that you never thought to hack your own cyber systems so you could communicate with Roingroing or anyone else, until I was in real trouble?"

"Huh? Oh yes. Kind of like there was some block in my cyber-neural programming that prevented me from even considering the idea. I needed an extreme situation to break through that. Almost like...the Agency didn't want me going there...."

"Exactly. And how scary to think they would mess with your mind and will like that! Makes me wonder what other not-so-ethical things they might have done—or are doing. That should be a chilling reminder that there's always the potential for corruption and tyranny with any secrecy. No, there needs to be full transparency. Starting with us, by making public all documents and intelligence on what just happened with Leonore and the governments and everything else."

Roingroing seemed startled. "But won't that caussse widessspread panic? You sssaid ssso in your concernsss about revealing yourssself to the whole galaxsssy."

"Maybe, to start with, for a short while. Or maybe not. I think intelligent beings can actually handle the truth better than we think, when given full information—unedited and unbiased and from all sides. Anyway, who are we to decide what anyone gets to know or not know? Who is *anyone* to make that call for everyone else?"

"Sounds very noble and lofty," Gates said. "But is it practical?"

"Is it any less practical than what we have now? No one should be kept in the dark about anything affecting them or their lives or their liberty. In fact, I think such an organizational overhaul could even serve as a model for the governments as well."

"Whoa. That's a big ask!"

"True. Government and bureaucratic inertia are very real. But it has to start with us, with a grassroots movement. Oh sure, it will be a struggle. We'll be going against the lowest aspects of human nature, or most any other species' nature for that matter, which always likes to arrange things in power hierarchies. And there will always be selfish and corrupt individuals—or self-righteous 'morally superior' ones—who seek to dominate others for their own agenda or personal advancement. It's unfortunately true that 'The price of freedom is eternal vigilance.' But with good people upholding and defending the cooperative agreements embodied in the galactic covenants, who recognize the advantages of working together for mutual benefit, the effort and the end will be worth it for all sentient beings everywhere."

"Wow. Waxing a little melodramatic there, aren't we?"

"Am I? Maybe so. Maybe I'm still exhausted from the ordeal I've been through. Or maybe I'm just fed up with the irrational idiocies of people and governments everywhere. If the Council wants my advice, that's fine. In fact, maybe that's all we should have: advisors, and members who decide on everything together. No more heads of anything, or ranks. Respect for knowledge and ability, yes, streamlined decision making in times of crisis, sure—as long as it adheres to the galactic covenants—but that's all."

Roingroing said thoughtfully, "I think you've jussst proven why you ssshould be head of the Councsssil."

"Nope, not a chance. Anyway, that's all hypothetical. Besides, even if the Council changes, the governments aren't likely to do so nearly as easily."

"Speaking of that," Gates put in, "you'll be interested to know that the balding guy and his faction who gave us so much grief, who pushed the nuclear attack through the government assembly, have lost favor among the other representatives. They've been censured and relegated to lesser status. It appears they won't be causing any trouble for a good while to come."

"What do you know! That's a start. Maybe this whole episode was enough to shake things up and get them to rethink how they run things, after all. Or at least lean in that direction. One can hope."

Gates cocked his head as if listening to an outside sound. "Someone else is here to see you."

The door slid open again and a small garden-gnome figure in a belted flight jacked strode in.

"Trix!" Jeanne exclaimed.

Trix put her hands on her hips. "Didn't think you were going to get away from me that easily, did you?"

Jeanne smiled broadly. "I'm glad you came. Gives me a chance to thank you in person more fully."

"From what I hear its all of us that should be thanking you. So you just concentrate on getting well and leave the rest to someone else for the time being. Forget whatever prattle these chuckleheads have been filling your ears with. That's all for the future."

"Good advice, Trix, as always. Can you stick around awhile?"

"Oh, I'm not going anywhere. I still have a fare to collect, you know. For me *and* my fellow pilots. And believe me, it's going to be a doozy!"

Epilogue

The engraved ever-steel plaque mounted on a pedestal at the entrance to the Spraang consulate in Lusteer read:

On this spot the first Citizen Advisor to the All-Species Council of Inter-Galactic Goodwill, Ambassador Jeanne (aka Astra Woman), along with her loyal partner Gates, sub-attaché Roingroing (later consul general Roingroing), the Gu'gundreans and the forest people of this world of Lystrom Two, working together in unwavering commitment to life, liberty, equal opportunity and respect for all, and without regard for their own wellbeing, first joined forces to save the galaxy from obliteration and the universe from tyranny at the hands of would-be overlord Leonore Squag.

This memorial is dedicated to the highest ideals, principles and practices that their efforts represent and inspire in all of us, as summarized in First Citizen Advisor Jeanne's often-stated motto: "Live and let live."

Leave A Review

If you enjoyed this sojourn into speculative fiction, please be kind enough to leave a review. That helps since reviews are used to rank books for other readers to see.

If you don't know where to do that you can search for this book by title or by ISBN number (that's this number: 979-8-9919780-0-2).

While you're at it you can check out my other titles!

Many thanks in advance! —WDB

About the Author

Wade D. Brown is an ex-navy man (navigation and hazardous-detail helm), writer, musician, fitness instructor, small business supervisor, corporate administrative manager, entrepreneur, ESL instructor, and most recently a caregiver for the developmentally disabled. He has an educational background in physics and the natural sciences, English composition, music, and art.

As a scientific generalist rather than a specialist, he has kept abreast of developments in a wide variety of fields, from neuroscience to genetics, quantum physics to cosmology, space flight to planetary ecology, information theory to psychology, cultural anthropology to sociobiology, health and nutrition to meditation and consciousness raising. His other activities include playing jazz guitar and piano, fitness, tennis, martial arts, and investigating spirituality by developing his own method of meditation using the scientific experimental method.

He draws strongly upon his experiences aboard three different navy ships and two WESTPAC deployments, as well as his background in the sciences, for authenticity to his stories of the future and shipboard life in space.

Besides his overseas travels while in the Navy to Southeast Asia, the Philippines, Hong Kong, Taiwan, Singapore, Pakistan, New Zealand—from which he developed an abiding interest in and respect for other cultures and ways of being—he has also lived in Honolulu, Los Angeles, San Diego, Madison (Wisconsin), Clearwater (Florida), and recently returned to his home town of Eau Claire, Wisconsin to devote time to his writing.

Wade adds: For more about me, or to see my other titles, upcoming releases, and personal gripes, pet peeves and rantings, visit **my Author Home Page** at:
https://sites.google.com/view/wade-d-brown-author/

or scan QR code: